FROM THE
NANCY DREW FILES

THE CASE: Nancy investigates an anonymous threat to write the last chapter in a romance writer's life.

CONTACT: In her next book, Esme Moore promises to tell all . . . which may be too much for her own good.

SUSPECTS: Todd Gilbert—*His ex-wife, Esme, taught him that romance is sweet. Has he now learned that revenge is sweeter?*

Giancarlo—*Esme's current husband says he'll love her to the end of time. But from the way he flirts with other women, perhaps the end is near.*

Kim Scott—*Yearning to be a writer, she envies Esme's success. She may lack talent, but she has no shortage of bitterness and bad feeling.*

COMPLICATIONS: It's almost Valentine's Day, and Ned's away at college. Surely he would understand why Nancy's sharing the case with detective Sam Fanelli. He might not be so understanding about all those slow dances, though. . . .

Books in The Nancy Drew Files™ Series

Available from ARCHWAY Paperbacks

The NANCY DREW Files™ 104

KISS AND TELL

CAROLYN KEENE

AN ARCHWAY PAPERBACK
Published by POCKET BOOKS

New York   London   Toronto   Sydney   Tokyo   Singapore

This book is a work of fiction. Names, characters, places and incidents are products of the author's imagination or are used fictitiously. Any resemblance to actual events or locales or persons, living or dead, is entirely coincidental.

AN ARCHWAY PAPERBACK *Original*

An Archway Paperback published by
POCKET BOOKS, a division of Simon & Schuster Inc.
1230 Avenue of the Americas, New York, NY 10020

ISBN: 0-671-88195-7

First Archway Paperback printing February 1995

10 9 8 7 6 5 4 3 2 1

NANCY DREW, AN ARCHWAY PAPERBACK and colophon
are registered trademarks of Simon & Schuster Inc.

THE NANCY DREW FILES is a trademark
of Simon & Schuster Inc.

Cover art by Cliff Miller

Printed in the U.S.A.

IL 6+

KISS AND TELL

Chapter

One

Do I look okay?" Nancy Drew's friend Bess Marvin asked. "I mean—do I really look okay?" Bess straightened her black velvet choker and pushed back a strand of blond hair.

"You look terrific!" Nancy said as they pulled away in Nancy's blue Mustang. "Gosh, Bess, you'd think you were going on a date with a hot new guy instead of to a book signing at a stuffy downtown hotel. If I didn't know how much you love romance novels, I'd wonder what had gotten into you."

Bess had pulled down the sun visor and looked in the mirror to examine her makeup. After reapplying a coat of Fabulous Grape lip gloss, Bess turned to address her friend. "Nancy Drew, you know Esme Moore just happens to be the hottest romance writer going, and this is a very

1

special occasion. Esme hasn't been home to River Heights for years. And she's planned an incredible few days to celebrate her home-coming."

Nancy negotiated a turn and whipped onto the expressway headed toward downtown River Heights. Once she'd gotten them safely into the flow of traffic, Nancy smoothed her reddish blond hair back behind her ears and said, "What exactly is planned?"

"Well—you won't be disappointed," Bess said mysteriously. She rummaged around in her purse and brought out a well-thumbed brochure that had a bright red heart on its cover. "Esme Moore's new book is called *Passion,* and it's being released this weekend, in time for Valen-tine's Day." Bess's sigh was full of longing and despair. "What I wouldn't give to have a date on Valentine's Day this year!" Bess said, forgetting to tell Nancy the weekend plans.

Nancy smiled her understanding. Bess had fallen hard for Kyle Donovan, an assistant in Nancy's father's law office, but Kyle was now in law school, and Bess rarely got to see him. Besides, when Kyle left to start school, he and Bess had agreed that the mature thing would be for them to cool their relationship. They visited each other occasionally, and they dated other people. Still, Bess hadn't met anyone who set her heart pounding as Kyle did!

"I've been there," Nancy said reassuringly.

2

"Oh, Nan," said Bess, her blue eyes reflecting her concern. "I should have remembered. You of all people know what it's like to keep up a long-distance romance. Maybe Ned will surprise you for Valentine's Day."

Nancy became pensive at the thought of her boyfriend, Ned Nickerson. Since he went to Emerson College, Nancy only got to see him on vacations and holidays. Unfortunately, Valentine's Day was neither. It hadn't been easy for Ned and Nancy to maintain a long-distance relationship, and there had been times when their feelings for each other had been put to the test, but throughout it all they managed to remember how important they were to each other. Until recently, that is. Lately, she and Ned had been fighting a lot, and Valentine's Day was the cause of one of their fights. Ned was busy with a big research paper and wanted Nancy to come to Emerson for a visit, but Nancy had promised Bess to go to Esme Moore's book signing. She didn't want to cancel out on her friend. The last time she talked to Ned about it, he'd been hurt and disappointed, and Nancy felt bad about letting him down. Still, there was nothing she could do. She'd promised Bess.

"Do you think he'll surprise you?" Bess pressed.

Shaking herself out of her reverie, Nancy went back to paying attention to the light early-afternoon traffic. "I'm afraid not, Bess," she said, starting off the exit ramp. "Ned's got a paper due next week, so he'll be grinding away all weekend."

"Kyle's the same way," said Bess with a laugh. "Even he didn't expect law school to be so tough." For a moment Nancy glimpsed the sadness on her friend's face and understood how hard the separation was for Bess. A moment later, though, Bess's face brightened and she was checking her makeup one last time. *"If* I happen to meet some gorgeous guy today, and *if* he happens to be interested in me, and *if* I like him, too, do me a favor, Nan."

"What's that?" Nancy asked.

"Remind me not to get serious about him," Bess stated flatly. "Kyle Donovan was it for me. I am never, I repeat never, getting serious about another guy again! It hurts too much when it gets complicated."

"I know, Bess, and don't worry, I'll remind you," Nancy promised.

Nancy was familiar with the hotel where Esme Moore was holding her book signing, because her father, Carson Drew, had his law offices nearby. Esme had a full schedule of events at the Barrington Hotel to celebrate the release of *Passion* and her birthday, which just happened to fall on Valentine's Day, Bess explained. Both girls drew in a sharp breath as they pulled into the Barrington's sweeping, circular driveway. Limousines lined the way, and the hotel's doormen and porters were busily escorting well-dressed guests and all their luggage through the brass-accented revolving doors.

"Wow," said Bess. "Esme sure has rich friends. Are we dressed up enough?"

"For a book signing?" Nancy asked. "I should hope so. Who are all these people anyway?"

Bess stepped out of the car, smoothed her green velvet dress under her wool plaid coat, and nervously fingered the choker at her throat. "Esme's a star, Nancy," Bess said. "With star power."

Nancy buttoned her green coat and gave the valet her keys before joining Bess at the hotel entrance. Just ahead of them an attractive blond woman turned to the man she was with and said, "Do you think Giancarlo will be here?"

"Does she go anywhere without her mascot?" the man shot back. The two broke out in laughter and headed for the registration desk.

"Did you see who that was?" Bess whispered at Nancy after the couple was gone. At Nancy's blank look, Bess rolled her eyes and said, "Lee Michelle! Esme's archrival. I can't believe she's here. And look—" Bess pointed out a tall, brown-haired man at the elevators. "That's Todd Gilbert."

"Not *the* Todd Gilbert," Nancy said.

"The one and only," Bess said, watching Todd disappear into an elevator. "I read in *Faces* magazine that Todd's trying for a comeback—with a part in the movie version of *Telling All,* Esme's soon-to-be-released autobiography."

Nancy nodded almost without thinking. Bess had been filling her ears with Esme trivia since she'd found out that her favorite romance writer was coming to River Heights. Along with Esme's novel *Passion,* her autobiography, *Telling All,* was to be published soon. The author was still making last-minute revisions to the autobiography, but already there was intense interest in the book, both from the public and from the various people Esme had known and about whom she was writing.

"I bet this place is full of people who would love to get their hands on a copy of that manuscript," Bess said. "Esme's promising to tell the truth, the whole truth, and nothing but the truth. There are a lot of powerful people who wish she'd lie about them—at least just a little!"

"Look," Nancy said, pointing to a dark-haired woman striding purposefully through the lobby.

"Brenda Carlton!" Bess said. "Two guesses what she's doing here."

Nancy shrugged. "Her father must have sent her to cover the event for *Today's Times.*"

"Watch out," Bess warned. "She's coming our way."

A moment later Brenda Carlton was standing next to them, flashing both Bess and Nancy a huge smile. "Surprise, surprise. I suppose you're here for the same reason I am?"

"If it's to see Esme Moore, then yes," Bess offered grudgingly.

Brenda's green eyes shone as she flipped back

her black hair to announce, "Well, guess who has a hot lead on Ms. Esme Moore?"

"It wouldn't be you, Brenda, would it?" Nancy said, raising an eyebrow.

"None other," Brenda said smugly. She tapped her pencil on the journalist's notebook she carried and checked her watch. "Unfortunately, I don't have time to stand around and brag. The book signing's supposed to start any minute. See you there! I'll be the one with the shocking revelation."

Bess narrowed her blue eyes as Brenda walked away. "I don't even want to think about the sleazy things she's up to."

"Lighten up, Bess," said Nancy. "Brenda may go overboard some times, but she's helped us out on a few occasions, too."

"I guess," Bess admitted. "Don't ask me to like her, though."

Nancy laughed, happy for her friend's loyalty. Because Nancy was a talented detective and Brenda was a reporter for her father's newspaper, they had gone up against each other more than once, matching investigative skills. Nancy was levelheaded and cautious. Brenda was impulsive and not always careful to check her facts.

"Come on," Bess urged. "Esme's book signing is about to start."

Bess led Nancy through the hotel lobby and along a plush, carpeted hall. The Barrington had undergone a million-dollar renovation recently, and it showed. The rich, dark paneling had been refinished and the bronze detailing had been polished until it gleamed. On the ceiling, original frescoes from the late nineteenth century were restored, and angels lit the way from on high.

In the sun-room the opulence became more intimate. Oversize sofas and armchairs, upholstered in rich browns and reds, were set among expensive antiques. Bay windows lined three sides of the room, and the late-afternoon sunlight cast a warm glow on the oil paintings hanging on the walls. Out the window the room faced an enormous garden. The overall effect was understated but elegant.

"Hurry!" Bess pushed Nancy forward into the crowd. "Esme should be here any minute. I don't want to get stuck at the back."

Sure enough, a blond-haired woman dressed in a tailored winter white suit was at the lectern, calling the crowd to attention. Around them, Nancy spotted several well-known faces, including those of Todd Gilbert and Esme's rival, Lee Michelle. Nancy couldn't believe that Esme could attract people like Vanessa Hopkins, the hot model, but there she was, along with her new husband, the rocker Billy Bolt. The couple were sitting next to Jesse Dean, the younger brother of the actor Jackson Dean, and an up-and-coming star himself. It seemed that everywhere she turned, Nancy spotted an actor or musician or writer.

"It's like being at an incredible nightclub,"

Bess marveled, her blue eyes wide with delight. "Wow!"

Nancy had to agree. "You were right, Bess. Esme is a star, with real star power."

"I told you," Bess said.

"Please take a seat," the blond-haired woman urged. "There are several comfortable sofas and armchairs up front."

Bess and Nancy sat in the front row. The woman at the lectern introduced herself as Janine Halpern, Esme's publicist. After giving a short introduction in which she highlighted some of the major successes of Esme's career, Janine finished, "But enough about her accomplishments. Let's have you meet the woman herself—in person."

The sun-room's double doors opened and Esme entered, followed by a stunningly handsome man and a younger woman in black. Esme was dressed in flowing red pants and a matching red silk shirt. At her throat, she wore a double strand of pearls. She strode into the room smiling and confident, her green eyes shining and her dark, shoulder-length hair swinging.

"Hello, everybody," Esme said into the microphone, her voice deep and husky. "I see some dear friends here, and I want to thank you all for coming." Esme reached over to the stack of books on the table beside her, picked one up, and held it aloft. The red and gold cover of *Passion* glinted as Esme showed it to the crowd. "This

9

one is hot!" she said, laughing lightly. "Please don't be shy about coming up to have me sign a copy for you. I promised Janine I'd start by answering questions. Who's first?"

A tall, brown-haired girl wearing jeans and a denim jacket stood up and said, "Uh, I was wondering. Is Giancarlo your husband?"

The man who'd come into the room with Esme smiled, displaying perfect white teeth and high cheekbones. He stood up in the front row, ran a hand through his hair, a mass of dark curls, and said in a softly accented voice, "I am indeed."

"Did you have a question for Giancarlo?" Esme asked graciously.

The girl stammered and blushed. "Uh-um, no, not really. I thought I recognized him from his picture. That's all."

Esme smiled and said, "Sometimes Giancarlo gets more attention than I do, but I don't mind. I realize he's a lot better looking!"

The crowd laughed. Giancarlo blew Esme a kiss and sat back down. Esme answered several more questions, some of them about *Passion* and how she came to write it, others about *Telling All* and when it would appear. Nancy found herself mesmerized by the woman—her charm, her grace, how she put everyone at ease. She had expected that someone as glamorous as Esme might be a little fake, but the opposite was true.

Bess, meanwhile, was in seventh heaven. She hung on the woman's every word, laughing at her every little joke. Nancy could tell that Bess would be first in line to buy a signed copy of *Passion*.

Janine was about to call an end to the questions when Nancy saw Brenda Carlton leap from her seat, notebook in hand. "Ms. Moore," Brenda shouted. "The publicity for your autobiography makes a lot of the fact that the book will be the truth, with no holds barred. Is that a fair characterization?"

Esme smiled ruefully and scanned the crowd. "There are some people here who would prefer I didn't tell the truth, but, yes, *Telling All* will be absolutely honest."

"Then why is there a rumor in New York that *Telling All* is going to be a big disappointment?" Brenda pressed.

"I don't know what you're talking about," Esme said, bristling.

"For example—" Brenda checked her notebook. "Will you tell the real truth about your ex-business partner Barry Hobbes? Or your relationship with Todd Gilbert and why it ended? Or the secrets you know about your rival, Lee Michelle?"

Esme stood her ground. "You pretend to know a lot about me. Who are you?"

"Brenda Carlton, *Today's Times.*"

"Well, Brenda, I suggest you do some fact-checking the next time you ask rude and unprofessional questions," Esme said.

Nancy held her breath. Brenda had bluffed her

way through a lot of situations, but Esme Moore was obviously a pro. She stood beside the lectern, her green eyes narrowed on Brenda.

"What's Brenda talking about?" Bess whispered.

"I think we're going to find out," Nancy said.

"You have five seconds to explain your comments," Esme pressed.

"I'd be happy to." Brenda lowered her notebook and turned her gaze to Esme herself. "I have a reliable source who swears that *Telling All* is nothing but lies. What do you have to say to that?"

Chapter

Two

I'M NOT GOING to sink to your level to answer unsubstantiated rumors," Esme said calmly, glaring at Brenda Carlton.

"Do you deny the accusation?" Brenda demanded.

Although she was restraining herself, Esme was obviously on the verge of losing her composure. Nancy felt the crowd grow restless. Flashes went off as photographers captured Esme's stony expression. After Brenda's accusation, the audience had let out a collective audible gasp, and now they were starting to talk among themselves. Esme knew she was losing her audience.

"Nancy, we've got to do something," Bess urged. "We can't let Brenda stand there and ruin Esme's reputation."

While Brenda went on, pressing Esme for an

13

answer, Nancy assumed Janine would jump in to stop her. The publicist only nodded and waited patiently for Brenda to ask every one of her questions, leaving Esme utterly vulnerable. When Brenda was done, Janine stood up at the podium and said, "We have heard these accusations before. They are untrue. Unlike Esme's other books, *Telling All* will not be a work of fiction!"

"Esme! Esme!" a photographer called out. When the author turned his way, the man caught Esme at her angriest and most vulnerable. More reporters jumped up from their seats around the perimeter of the room and demanded an explanation for Brenda's accusation. Janine shouted for the audience to compose itself. All the while, Nancy watched Esme draw deep breaths, obviously trying to calm herself.

Bess was right. Nancy couldn't just sit by and let the chaos continue. "Come on," she said to Bess. "We need to stop this at the source."

With that, Nancy led the way to where Brenda was standing. When the young reporter saw Bess and Nancy, her green eyes flashed—in fear or surprise, Nancy couldn't tell—but she promptly put her notebook away.

"I'd like to ask *you* a few questions, Brenda," Nancy stated flatly.

"Such as?" Brenda asked.

Nancy crossed her arms and eyed the reporter suspiciously. "Who's your source?" Nancy demanded. "You and I both know that as a responsible journalist, you can't go around making accusations without confirmation from at least two sources."

A flicker of fear passed over Brenda's face, and Nancy knew her suspicions were well founded. Brenda was obviously on a fishing expedition, and probably had nothing more than rumors to back up her questions.

"I've got a source," Brenda insisted, her eyes narrowed to show her determination. "Someone who swears to have proof that Esme Moore's autobiography is"—Brenda checked her notebook and read from a page—"here it is: 'Esme Moore is a fake, and that book of hers is a pack of lies.' That's a direct quote."

"From whom?" Bess demanded, reaching for Brenda's notepad.

"None of your business!" Brenda cried. She shoved the notebook back into her black bag.

The crowd had quieted down, and Esme was actually signing books. The reporters had cornered Janine, and Brenda, sensing that was where the action was, gathered up her coat and followed.

"There goes trouble," said Bess. "I've seen that fire in Brenda's eyes before, and I never like what comes of it. Why is she going after Esme?" Bess wailed. "She's a great person and doesn't need trouble from someone like Brenda Carlton."

"It's not Brenda who's going after Esme,"

Nancy told her friend. "Brenda's source is the person who wants to get at Esme. The question is, who and why?"

While Bess got in line to buy a copy of Esme's book and have it signed, Nancy sat down and waited for her friend. Something nagged at her about Brenda's questions and Esme's responses. Then she remembered what it was: Janine had said that they were aware of the accusations and rumors. So Brenda's line of questioning wasn't new to them. If Nancy was right, someone had already been after Esme. Therefore Brenda's questioning could be part of a larger attempt to ruin Esme's reputation by branding her a liar.

When Bess came back, a signed copy of *Passion* in her hand and stars in her eyes, Nancy shared her suspicions with her friend. Bess's stars immediately dimmed.

"We've got to help her, Nan," Bess urged. "Let's tell Esme we want to find out who's been spreading these rumors."

"My idea exactly," said Nancy. "But will Esme want our help? My guess is that she or her publisher has already investigated the rumors."

"Maybe," Bess said. "Maybe not. We don't know till we ask!"

In a little while Esme finished signing her books and, along with Giancarlo, Janine, and the young girl in black, left the room. Photographers packed up their equipment and hotel staff busied themselves rearranging the sofas and chairs.

Nancy and Bess made their way from the room to the main desk, where they found out Esme's room number. In the elevator up to the sixth floor, where Esme had a suite, Nancy made a mental list of the questions she'd ask the woman if Esme agreed to let her investigate.

"How long have they been going on?" Nancy asked herself. "And how did they start? Phone calls? Notes? Is your publisher aware of the situation? If so, has he or she done anything to find out who's behind the rumors?"

"Nancy." Bess prodded her friend in the side with her finger and glanced around the elevator. Several passengers smiled at the two girls. "You're talking to yourself."

"I was thinking," Nancy whispered back.

"Out loud," Bess informed her, a wide smile spreading across her face. "It's because you're excited to be on a case," Bess remarked. "That way you don't have to spend Valentine's Day alone. You can spend it with a mystery!"

On the sixth floor, Nancy and Bess found Esme's corner suite at the end of a long corridor. The door was closed, but when Nancy knocked it was quickly opened by Giancarlo. "May I help you girls?" he asked in his softly accented voice.

Up close, Giancarlo was even more handsome, with his flashing blue eyes and long, thick eyelashes. Bess stood tongue-tied, but Nancy managed to introduce them both, and said, "We'd like to speak to Esme if it's possible."

"In reference to what, may I ask?" Giancarlo said, clearly used to putting off Esme's fans.

"It's about the questions that reporter was asking," Nancy offered. "We're hoping, I mean, we were thinking—"

"Nancy's a detective," Bess blurted out, suddenly rediscovering her ability to speak.

"Is she?" Giancarlo asked skeptically.

"Giancarlo, where are you?" a woman's voice asked.

"I'm talking to a detective," Giancarlo answered, speaking over his shoulder. When he turned back to Nancy, his blue eyes were sparkling, and there was a small grin tugging at the corners of his mouth.

"A what?" the woman cried.

"There's a young woman here who apparently wants to sign on as your personal private investigator," he said. "What should I tell her?"

"Tell her I'm not interested." Esme Moore herself appeared at the door. When she saw Nancy and Bess standing there, she appeared to be taken aback and surprised. "Which one of you is the detective?" she asked.

Nancy grinned and quickly found her nerve as she dove into an explanation of how she and Bess knew Brenda Carlton and suspected that someone was using her to make the accusations against Esme.

"Nancy wants to investigate," Bess put in.

"If you're willing," Nancy said. "I've had a bit

of experience and some luck with this sort of investigation in the past."

Both Esme and Giancarlo seemed amused, but Nancy could tell Esme was weighing the idea seriously. "Why don't you come in?" she suggested. "Janine's downstairs, but when she comes back we can all talk."

Like the lobby downstairs, Esme's suite was paneled in rich mahogany with bronze fixtures. The living room was furnished with antiques, and through an open door Nancy saw that the bedroom had a huge four-poster bed. Esme sat down on a flowered sofa, while Giancarlo pulled up armchairs for the girls.

"If there is a problem," Nancy said gently once they were seated, "I honestly believe I can help."

Esme paused. She still seemed a bit reticent to tell Nancy her problems, but finally the writer nodded, pushed back her dark hair, and said, "As Janine said downstairs, someone has been spreading rumors and gossip—malicious gossip —about *Telling All.* The claims are that the book is pure fabrication and that I shy away from telling inside stories about people and events. Further, they go on to accuse me of hiding behind lies. What makes these rumors so offensive is that I only agreed to write the book because everyone urged me to set the record straight about certain events in my life. People want the truth, and that's what I plan to give them."

"Don't let yourself get upset, *cara*," Giancarlo urged, sitting on the couch beside her. "Janine says you should simply ignore the threats."

"Threats?" Nancy asked. "What kind of threats?"

Esme sighed. "Someone has been sending notes to my publisher, warning me against publishing the book and threatening to ruin my career if I go ahead with *Telling All*."

"That's terrible," Bess said. "Who would do such a thing?"

"I don't know," Esme confessed. "Someone who wants to ruin me obviously."

"Maybe I can help you find out," said Nancy.

A knock sounded at the door, and Giancarlo went to answer it. Nancy was about to ask Esme more about the threats when a man's shout broke the silence from the open front door.

"I will so see her!" the man cried. "Let me in, you—"

Nancy turned in her chair to see Giancarlo trying to force the door closed. Whoever was on the other side had stuck his foot beside the door frame and was doing his best to push the door open. Finally Giancarlo wasn't strong enough to hold off the intruder. As soon as the door flew all the way open, Esme cried out, "Todd! What are you doing here?"

Nancy recognized Todd Gilbert from the book signing downstairs. His light brown hair was disheveled from his struggle, and he had loosened his necktie.

"I need to see you," Todd said, striding purposefully into the room.

"Too bad," Giancarlo said.

Esme's husband blocked his way, and before Todd could react, Giancarlo whipped his arm back and took a gigantic swing at the actor, knocking him to the floor.

Chapter

Three

Nᴀɴᴄʏ ᴄᴏᴜʟᴅ ᴛᴇʟʟ that Todd Gilbert was going to have a nice black eye the next day. The actor moaned, clutched his head, and rose to a sitting position.

"Thanks a bundle," he managed to say. "I was going to have new head shots taken this afternoon. There goes that plan."

"You have no right to be here," Giancarlo said, standing over Todd. "If you don't leave immediately, I may be forced to strike you again."

"Please—" Esme said, holding up her hand for peace. She walked over to Todd and Giancarlo. "There's no need for this kind of display."

"I thought you never wanted to see him again," Giancarlo protested.

Esme sighed. "I didn't mean for you to defend me with your fists, *caro.*" She held out a hand to

Todd and helped him up from the floor. "Can't we settle this like adults?"

While Esme spoke to Todd and Giancarlo in low tones, Nancy remembered some of the gossip Bess had told her about the actor. His career took a nosedive after he and Esme had broken up a few years earlier. He'd been trying to make a comeback ever since, but his career floundered after he had become known as being difficult and short-tempered.

Bess whispered to her that Todd had been trying to change his image into that of a sensitive male type. "He even wears glasses sometimes," Bess said. "Like that's going to convince anyone."

Nancy laughed softly. "If this scuffle is any indication, he's going to need more than glasses to overcome his reputation," Nancy said.

Esme had sent Todd and Giancarlo out of the room and asked that they not come back until they had settled their differences.

"Men!" Esme said, flopping back down on the sofa. Despite all her cool glamour, when Esme smiled she looked as if she were in her twenties. "Can't live with them, can't live without them."

"I hear you," Bess said.

"I hope you aren't disappointed, now that you've seen the private Esme Moore," the romance writer said. "Todd and Giancarlo are jealous of each other. I'm afraid it's not entirely over me."

"What do you mean?" Nancy asked.

"They both want a part in the movie version of *Telling All.* I've got a deal in the works with a Hollywood production company. Todd's read for the role of my editor in the movie version. As far as I'm concerned, if he gets cast he can be in the film, but I prefer not to have anything to do with him. I won't stand in the way of his career, though. Meanwhile, Giancarlo has been cast to play himself, and he's vetoed the idea of Todd's having a part. He says if Todd's in it, he won't be." Esme shrugged. "I'm a writer, not a magician. It's up to them to settle their differences."

The door to the suite opened. Nancy expected to see Todd and Giancarlo, but instead Janine Halpern came in, along with a young woman in black who wore funky, thick-soled shoes and rings on all her fingers. Nancy remembered seeing the young woman earlier at the book signing. From where she sat curled up on the couch, Esme introduced Nancy and Bess.

"Janine Halpern, my publicist, and Kim Scott, my assistant," Esme said. "This is Nancy Drew and Bess Marvin. Janine, these girls want to help us find out who's spreading those rumors."

Kim's dark eyes flashed as she crossed the room and picked up the phone. While she dialed, she expressed her surprise. "Really?"

"Nancy's a detective," Esme explained. With a shrug she said to Janine, "What do you think? My publisher hasn't made any headway on those threatening notes. Why don't we let Nancy have a crack at them?"

Janine deliberated for a moment, checking out Nancy and Bess with an intense, thin-lipped expression. Before she had a chance to answer, Esme added, "They know that reporter who was asking those questions earlier. What's her name?"

"Brenda Carlton," Bess offered.

"From *Today's Times,*" Janine finished. "I just spent the last ten minutes fielding her questions, along with those of five other reporters. Frankly, Esme, if it's the reporters who are bothering you, I've told you before that I wouldn't worry about any publicity that comes from this. In our business, there's no such thing as bad news."

Esme returned Janine's steady gaze. "And I told you that I'm not interested in having some nut case out there trying to ruin the reputation I've spent fifteen years building."

Nancy was about to speak up when Kim, off the phone now, announced, "They're sending up hot water for your tea and a plate of raw vegetables. Did you want anything else?"

"Nothing right now," Esme told her. "I'll give you a call if I need you."

"No problem." With a toss of her dark hair, Kim walked toward the door. "I'll be in my room. Ciao!"

After Kim left, Nancy spoke to Janine. "Whether or not the publicity is good for Esme, harassment is illegal. Since Esme is willing to let us investigate, I'd like to peek at the notes she's gotten."

With a sigh, Janine opened the briefcase she had with her and handed over a file to Nancy. "Those are all the notes that have been received, including the envelopes. Please be careful. Although I left copies at my office in New York, these are the originals."

Nancy took the file from Janine. "Before we leave, I'd like to know if you have any suspicions about who might be spreading these rumors? Who has the most to lose by what you've written?"

Esme shook her head sadly. "Whoever is most worried about the truth, I suppose."

"Was Brenda right?" Bess put in. *"Are* you writing about Lee Michelle and Barry Hobbes? Is Todd in the book?"

"All of them," Esme confirmed, her green eyes lighting up in amusement. "And others, too. But seriously, Nancy, there are many friends and enemies who have contacted me since I started writing the book, begging me to protect them and their reputations. I've told everyone that I'm not open to suggestion, bribery, or threats."

"Clearly someone hasn't gotten the message," Nancy said, putting the file in her purse. "I'm going to do my best to find out who that is."

Fifteen minutes later Nancy was heading home to pore through the file Janine had given her. She'd left Bess at Esme's hotel room, since the romance novelist had kindly agreed to answer some of Bess's questions about the business and how she might become a writer, too.

Nancy's father wasn't home from work, and a note from their housekeeper, Hannah Gruen, told Nancy she'd gone to the store. After checking the answering machine and finding no messages, Nancy climbed the stairs to her room, threw herself down on the bed, and started going through the file. An hour later she realized just how hard the case was going to be. Starting three months earlier, Esme, her publisher, her agent, even prominent reviewers and booksellers, had received dozens of threatening notes. Every single one was typewritten, but the typefaces were all different. Even worse, the notes were all mailed from different addresses across the Midwest. There was no way Nancy could travel to each post office. If she was going to trace the note writer, she would need help.

Starting with the various kinds of paper the notes were typed on, Nancy made a list of possible clues. Once she'd gotten to the end, her list read: "paper—eighteen different kinds; typefaces—twelve different kinds; addresses—fifteen." Letting out a long sigh, Nancy went back over each note, searching for telltale clues. Aside from some minor differences, the notes simply warned the person to whom they were addressed not to have anything to do with Esme's book— that it would be a pack of lies—and threatened that if Esme went ahead with the project, the note writer would make sure her career was ruined. They were all about the same except for the last one. The first time she read it, Nancy had gotten a shiver. Now, rereading it, she noticed something different, something she should have seen before.

"Black Widow," the note read, "I'm insulted. Since you've decided to ignore me, I'll have to make it personal. The threats will stop and the deeds will begin."

Why was the writer addressing Esme as Black Widow? Was this a clue Esme might recognize? Nancy picked up the phone and dialed the Barrington. Seconds later Esme's familiar husky voice came through the line.

"This is Esme Moore," she said.

Nancy quickly asked her about the reference to Black Widow. "Does it have some kind of special meaning?" she asked.

"My goodness," Esme said, "it certainly does. I'm surprised no one noticed that before. Even Janine knows that used to be my nickname."

"Your nickname?" Nancy echoed.

Esme gave a short bark of a laugh. "Back in my salad days I never wore anything but black. And I guess I tended to break men's hearts. So my closest friends all called me Black Widow."

"How many people in your immediate circle would know this nickname?" Nancy asked.

"Let me think." Esme paused. "There's Janine," she said, "and Kim. Giancarlo, of course. Todd. Nancy, you don't think it's someone I know—*personally?*"

"This note seems to indicate it is," Nancy said, but after hanging up with Esme, Nancy stared at the note for a long time, thinking to herself, "Someone who has a serious grudge, too."

The next morning Nancy picked Bess up early. Esme was holding a press conference at the Barrington since the event the day before had officially been a book signing.

At the coat check in the hotel, Bess barely had her coat off before she was scolding her friend. "Nancy, you haven't said a word about my outfit."

Bess was wearing flowing red pants and a matching shirt that were remarkably similar to the outfit Esme had worn the day before. "I ran out and bought it last night before the mall closed. What do you think?"

"I like it," Nancy said. "Red is a good color for you."

"Thanks!" Bess beamed. "Esme says women shouldn't shy away from red. It shows they have confidence and aren't afraid of their power."

"It sounds like Esme is full of good advice," Nancy said. "What does she say about jeans?" Nancy added, pointing out her own denim shirt and matching pants.

"That they make you look like a cowhand," Bess said with a laugh. "Come on, let's go."

The press conference was being held in a small room between the lobby and the sun-room. Bess led the way. "Hurry," she urged. "I don't want to miss a thing."

"Bess, we're early," Nancy insisted, checking

her watch. "The press conference isn't supposed to start until ten, and it's only nine-fifteen."

As soon as Nancy and Bess arrived at the room, they both realized that something was dreadfully wrong. Esme stood guard at the half-open door, frantic, while inside Nancy spotted Janine and Kim furiously scrambling around the room, tearing down posters that had decorated the walls.

"What happened?" Nancy asked.

"This." Esme said. Her green eyes brimming with tears, Esme threw open the door for them to see.

Inside, wherever there was a picture or poster of Esme, someone had scrawled the word *Liar* or *Fraud* across it in huge, red letters. Even worse was the banner that hung above the podium on which the phrase Coming Soon: Esme Moore Tells All had been changed to read Tells Lies!

"Find the person who did this," Esme said to Nancy, her voice high and thin with frustration and anger. "Find whoever is trying to ruin me— before he or she succeeds!"

Chapter

Four

WHILE JANINE AND KIM continued to clear the room of all the ruined press materials, Nancy surveyed the damage. Along with all the photographs and the banner, press kits and releases had to be thrown away, too. Until now this had been a case involving harassment, but with this act sabotage was involved. Nancy knew it was time to call the police.

Esme regained her composure after her initial outburst, and gave Nancy a frustrated and disgusted tour of the damage. "Who would do such a thing?" she asked, her pearl and diamond earrings glinting in the soft morning light. "My life and work are about romance and adventure and fantasy—about escaping this kind of ugliness and hatred. Why is this happening to me?"

31

"Esme!" a woman called out. Nancy turned to see a well-dressed, middle-aged couple approaching. The woman was tanned and fit and dressed in an expensive-looking gray cashmere blazer, a white silk blouse, and jeans. The man had on similar attire, and was carrying a briefcase on a strap over his shoulder. "Darling!" he said. "We've been searching all over for you. Our plane just got in. We're exhausted, but we couldn't wait to see you!"

"Bob, Helen," Esme said wearily. "I'm so glad you got here. Look at this mess. Look what someone did, and right before my press conference."

"What about our announcement?" Helen asked, fingering the ruined banner. "I'm sure you realize this is not good, Esme, not good at all."

Esme turned to Nancy and Bess to introduce them all. "Helen Klein and Bob Samuels are from Klein-Samuels Productions, the company that's going to make the movie version of *Telling All*. I hate to ruin the surprise, but we were going to use this press conference to announce that the film has been cast."

Bess could barely contain her excitement. Nancy saw she was itching to ask if Todd would be in the movie. Before she could say a word, Bob asked Esme, "Who are these girls?"

For a long moment Esme was silent and acted uncomfortable. Nancy could tell she was debating how much to reveal to Helen and Bob. Finally she took a deep breath and said, "Nancy is a detective. She and her friend Bess came for the press conference today and Nancy has kindly offered to help me find out who might be trying to make my life difficult." Esme didn't mention the notes or problems the night before. Clearly, she was playing it low key.

"Did she?" Helen Klein asked, giving Nancy a withering look. "Listen, Esme, I hate to be a wet blanket, but don't you think we should call the police? They're more *experienced* at this sort of thing."

Nancy cleared her throat. "Actually, I was planning to get in touch with my contacts in the River Heights Police Department."

Esme wanted to stop Nancy. "Do you really think we need to?"

Nancy and Helen Klein were on the same side. Simultaneously they both said, "Of course." Nancy offered to make the call, while Bess stayed behind to help Janine and Kim and Esme conferred with Helen and Bob. Nancy found a phone in the hotel lobby and quickly put in the call. B.D. Hawkins, Nancy's best contact, wasn't at his desk, so she had him paged. Even though B.D. was in Homicide, he could recommend someone on the force to help with their sabotage case.

"There's Jack Henley," B.D. said when Nancy told him what was going on. "But he's kind of a relic and I'm not sure you'd get along. Paula Jablonski—no. I got it! There's a new kid assigned here. Sam Fanelli. You'll love him. The guy's a crackup. He's cute, too."

"Thanks, B.D.," Nancy said. "But I don't care how cute he is, just that he's good."

"He was top of his class," B.D. assured her. "I'll put in the call to his superior right now. Hopefully, he's available. If not, I'll find someone else, don't worry."

Before heading back to the room, Nancy started some preliminary investigating. At the front desk, she questioned the day manager, a young woman named Terri, who put her onto the person in charge of all the conference and meeting rooms. When J.J. Vaz came to the front desk, Nancy told her about what had happened to Esme's press materials.

"I can't believe it," the woman said. "I was in there at eight and everything was fine. Then I made my rounds of the hotel from eight until nine, and then I took my breakfast break. I just got back."

So someone got in there between eight and nine, just before Esme, Janine, and Kim arrived, Nancy determined. "Was the door locked?" she asked.

J.J. shrugged and expressed her regret. "Unfortunately not. It's hotel policy to keep conference and meeting rooms locked, but Janine Halpern requested that it remain open so that early arrivals would be able to let themselves in. I told her she'd have to take responsibility if anything happened. I'm so sorry about this," J.J. said.

Back in the press room, there was little evidence, if any, of what had occurred. Bess, Janine, and Kim were rearranging the few press materials that had not been damaged, and Esme was cheerfully greeting the arriving guests, reporters, and photographers. Giancarlo had arrived, and was dressed to kill in an expensive gray wool suit. He stood by Esme as she said her hellos and posed dutifully for the cameras. Finally Janine called the press conference to order. One last person sneaked into the room before Janine closed the door. Janine greeted the late arrival with a cheerful hello and personally escorted her to an available seat. Nancy was shocked to see that it was Brenda.

Bess, who was standing with Nancy at the back of the room, didn't miss Janine's greeting. "Why is she suddenly so friendly to Brenda Carlton?" she whispered to Nancy.

"You got me," Nancy said, bells going off. Janine had asked that the press room remain unlocked. Janine had also said that no publicity was bad publicity. Now Janine was acting friendly toward Brenda Carlton, despite the fact that it was Brenda who'd been a nuisance at the book signing the day before. Plus she'd made no effort to stop Brenda during her attack.

As soon as Esme stood before the press podium, the room became quiet. "I'll take your questions in a moment," the romance writer said, her voice hushed and sultry. "But first, I have an important announcement to make." Esme paused. "Helen Klein and Bob Samuels have come to some final decisions about the cast for the movie version of *Telling All,"* Esme told the crowd. "I'm pleased to announce that Giancarlo will play the part of himself, my husband, and Todd Gilbert has been cast as my editor, Conrad O'Brien."

A murmur of surprise went through the crowd. As photographers snapped away, both Giancarlo and Todd came up to the podium to stand beside Esme. Todd was wearing tinted glasses that made him look more bookish but Nancy knew they were just a prop to hide what was probably a black eye. He was beaming for the photographers. Esme's husband, on the other hand, seemed to be furious about sharing the podium with Todd.

"He doesn't seem very happy," Bess said.

For the next half hour Esme, Todd, and Giancarlo answered questions from the press. During the conference, a young, good-looking guy let himself into the room and stood at the back near Bess and Nancy. He took a pad from the pocket of his tweed jacket and started jotting notes.

"Who's he?" Bess whispered to Nancy. "He's cute."

"I'm not sure," said Nancy.

The woman sitting next to Nancy dropped her purse on the ground. Nancy reached down to pick it up and hand it to her. The woman was wearing a big floppy hat with flowers on the brim and large eyeglasses.

36

"Thank you so much," the woman said in a refined voice. She had graying hair and smooth, pale skin. "Are you a fan of Esme?" she asked.

"Sort of," Nancy said. "My friend Bess is the one who reads romances. How about you?"

The woman crossed her long legs. "I'm one of Esme's oldest fans," she said in that same quiet, refined voice. "Pia Wieland." She reached out a gloved hand to introduce herself.

"Nancy Drew," said Nancy. "And this is my friend, Bess Marvin."

Bess smiled and nodded at Pia. By now, the conference was breaking up, and the good-looking guy in the tweed jacket and denim shirt approached Esme and Janine. Nancy saw Janine point in her direction, and the young man started over to them. Just as the guy approached, Nancy noticed Pia quietly leave the room.

"Detective Sam Fanelli," the man said, holding out his hand. "B.D. sent me."

B.D. had said that Sam was young, but Nancy hadn't expected someone who appeared to be her own age. He barely looked twenty, but Nancy knew he had to be at least twenty-five. Maybe it was his slow, shy smile, or the eager expression in his chocolate brown eyes, but Nancy found herself surprised to be talking to a police officer who felt more like a friend. With Bess filling in, Nancy quickly gave Sam the details of what had happened so far.

When Nancy was done, Sam looked over his notes, chewed on his lower lip, and said, "They trained us about the m.o.'s of stalkers and harassers. Usually these criminals seek revenge for imagined wrongs. Often they just want to ruin their victims' personal lives, that sort of thing. But they can also be dangerous. We can't be too careful here. Do you have those notes you mentioned?"

"No," said Nancy. "Since they're originals, I left them at home—just in case."

"Good," Sam said, his voice low and his expression intense. Then suddenly he smiled and said, "Can you tell I'm new to this duty? I've been practicing my serious voice on you."

Sam laughed and Nancy and Bess joined in. Nancy had to stop herself from thinking it could be fun to work with Sam. "I'll get you those notes," she told him. "Maybe you'll see something I might have missed."

Kim Scott came over, her arms full of press materials. "Esme has a photo shoot for the movie deal scheduled for after lunch. She told me you're welcome to come along if you want. We're going to take a limo from the hotel at noon."

"Thanks," Bess said. "We'll be there." Kim walked away and Bess asked, "Is that okay, Nancy? I mean, we can watch out for Esme that way."

"Sam and I should go over the notes," Nancy said, thinking aloud. "We only have about an hour until lunch."

"I can start on the notes while you and Bess are

at the shoot," Sam said. "That way, you can keep an eye on Esme."

"Great idea!" Bess cried.

Nancy hurried home to pick up the file Janine had given her before racing back to the hotel. Luckily, the traffic wasn't too bad, and she made the round trip in less than forty-five minutes. Bess and Sam were waiting for her when she got back beside two stretch limousines, which were lined up at the curb. Behind them was a beat-up compact. Nancy pulled alongside it to allow the valet to park her Mustang. Then she handed the notes to Sam, who took them with a smile.

"See ya," he said, climbing in behind the wheel of the compact. After he was gone, Nancy checked her watch and said, "We have time for a quick bite."

"I'm too excited to eat," Bess said. "Going to Esme's photo shoot—and in a limo!"

"Well, I'm starving," Nancy said. "There's a coffee shop across the street. I'll pick up a couple of sandwiches." By the time Nancy had ordered and paid for the two tuna salad sandwiches and iced teas to go, one limousine had already pulled away from the curb in front of the Barrington.

Bess was breathless when Nancy returned. "I thought you'd never get back," she said. "Esme and Janine have already left with Todd and Giancarlo. Kim's waiting for us."

Nancy and Bess stepped inside the spacious limousine and the driver closed the door behind them. Kim smiled, then gave the driver instructions to a photographer's studio across town. After that, she sat back and studied her fingernails the rest of the trip and didn't say another word.

When they arrived at the studio, they saw Esme already posing with Todd and Giancarlo. Janine was giving the photographer, a young woman in a white T-shirt, blue jeans, and cowboy boots, instructions on how to pose the three and which angles were Esme's best. Bess turned to Nancy and said, "Isn't this exciting?"

Nancy opened up her sandwich and began to eat, smiling at her friend's enthusiasm. Truthfully, she found the whole process pretty tedious. Every time Janine asked for another shot, the photographer and her assistant had to move the lights and reset the meters and the cameras. Then the camera would need to have a new roll of film and Janine would change her mind again and the whole thing would be repeated. For a while Nancy watched, but soon she was strolling around the spacious studio, checking out the various props and backdrops. She passed by the darkroom at one point and saw that the lights were on. Kim was chatting with the photographer's assistant, a young man in jeans, a black T-shirt, and a single hoop earring.

"I don't know why everyone doesn't just see right through her!" Kim cried. "I mean, she is so fake. Did you see her posing with Todd and

Giancarlo, like she's crazy about both of them? You want to know the truth?" she asked.

"Mmmm," the young man replied, evidently more worried about the film he was loading than Kim's complaints.

"The truth is, she can't stand Todd, and doesn't care a bit about Giancarlo. She's only out for herself—"

"Kim!" came Janine's voice. "We need that suitcase. Where is it?"

"Coming!" Kim replied.

Nancy darted out of sight as Kim scooted past her carrying a suitcase that Nancy remembered her having in the limousine. For a moment Nancy wondered why Kim hadn't just put the suitcase in Esme's dressing room. Kim strode over and handed Esme the suitcase. Apparently it contained a change of clothes, because by the time Nancy returned to Bess, Esme had gone off to the dressing room and Janine was scolding Kim for wandering off with Esme's change of clothes.

"If she doesn't like it, she can fire me," Nancy heard Kim grumble.

"She's got attitude," Bess whispered to Nancy.

"You don't know the half of it," Nancy said. She was about to pull Bess aside to tell her about what she'd overheard, when Esme's screams filled the studio.

"Help!" she cried. "Someone help!"

Nancy was the first to react. She raced to the

41

dressing room and frantically knocked on the door.

"Esme, it's Nancy. Are you okay?" she asked. "Is something wrong in there?"

Esme, who was still dressed, threw open the door and rushed out of the room. Her hair was disheveled, and her face contorted with fear.

"In my suitcase!" she cried, barely getting the words out. "There . . . there . . ."

"Esme, calm down," Janine said as she approached. She put her arm around the romance writer. "What's wrong?"

Carefully Nancy and Bess walked into the dressing room and stepped over to the suitcase. Then they saw what had made Esme so frantic. Nestled among the folds of Esme's white lace blouse, they spotted a black mound with eight hairy legs.

It was a deadly black widow spider.

Chapter

Five

LOOK AT THAT!" Esme said, pointing out the spider to Janine and Giancarlo. "They're poisonous. And they bite! Think of what could have happened to me."

Nancy started to slam the lid on the suitcase, but just before she did, she noticed a typewritten note in the suitcase: "How does it feel, Black Widow, to know you're a liar?"

With a shiver, Nancy pointed out the note to Esme. Now, the romance novelist let out another wail, one that brought Helen, Bob, Todd, and Kim to the dressing room.

"What's going on?" Helen asked. She took one glance at the distraught Esme and shot her partner a look of dismay. "Are you okay, dear?"

Esme quickly put up a hand and patted her hair, laughing nervously. "I must look like a mess. I was in the middle of changing when I found *that* in my suitcase. Needless to say, it gave me a shock!"

Nancy stepped back to let the group view the black widow spider before slamming the lid of the suitcase. "It can't hurt us now. What I'd like to know is, how did it get into Esme's suitcase?" Nancy made a point of directing her gaze at Kim as she asked the question.

Helen Klein smiled grimly. "I hope you find out, kid." She checked her watch and, giving her partner a knowing nod, said, "Bob, we'd better go if we don't want to miss that meeting."

"Right," Bob Samuels agreed. He pecked Esme on the cheek. "Keep a stiff upper lip, Es. We're going to need you to write that screenplay. Take care of her, G.C., would you?"

Giancarlo put his arm around Esme. "I intend to, you can be sure."

As soon as Helen and Bob left, Janine went off to give instructions to the photographer, leaving Nancy, Bess, Esme, Giancarlo, Kim, and Todd standing outside the dressing room.

"I think you've got a few questions to answer, young lady," Esme said to her assistant. "You were responsible for that suitcase. Would you care to explain how someone managed to slip a deadly spider—and a threatening note—inside it?"

Kim crossed her arms and narrowed her dark eyes on Esme. "Your guess is as good as mine," she said.

"That's no answer!" Esme cried.

After pouting, Kim then addressed the rest of the group. "After I packed the suitcase, I left it in Esme's room during the press conference. Where I *thought* it would be safe!"

"Obviously someone broke into Esme's hotel room during the press conference and put the spider inside the suitcase, or else it happened here at the studio," Nancy concluded.

"But that would mean it was one of us," Bess concluded.

"Don't look at me!" Todd protested. "I hate bugs."

"Kim, you had the suitcase with you once we arrived here," Esme pointed out.

There was an awkward silence. Esme stared at Kim, who started to say something but seemed to think better of it. She just turned and stalked away. Before she turned, Nancy thought she saw tears in the young woman's eyes.

"Kim!" Giancarlo cried. "Don't be that way!" He gave Esme an imploring look. "You know she wouldn't do such a thing. You should go apologize to her right now."

"Oh, please," Esme said with a sigh. "I pay her well enough. I don't have to apologize to her, too."

"You're a cold woman, Esme," Giancarlo said.

His eyes narrowed on her for a moment, and then he went after Kim, who had disappeared.

"Harsh words," Todd said lightly.

"You'd probably be the first to agree with him," Esme said, her lips trembling. Nancy felt as though she and Bess were about to witness something very private. She coughed lightly to remind Esme and Todd that they weren't alone. Then she edged away from them, trying to find a way to exit gracefully. She headed back toward the darkroom. Despite her obvious interest, Bess also did the diplomatic thing and turned her back on Esme and Todd, joining Nancy by the darkroom.

"I've told you, Esme, I take the blame for everything," Nancy heard Todd say. "If I thought you would ever forgive me, I'd be down on my hands and knees in a second. Why can't you believe it was someone else who did those things?"

"Todd, please." Esme took a long pause before continuing. "That's all in the past."

"But your book—" Todd protested.

"The book will tell only the truth," Esme countered. "No one can stop me from doing that."

"Think about what I asked you, Esme," Todd implored. "If you could simply hold back just a little . . . you and I both know it would help me out a lot." Todd's voice grew gentle. "We shared quite a bit," he said. "I find it hard to believe you can't remember our good times."

Esme let out a long sigh. "I do, Todd, I do. Please leave me alone now. So far, this hasn't been the greatest day."

"I understand," Todd said. "Will I see you tonight? Will you save a dance for the man who once had your heart?"

At this, Bess clutched Nancy's arm and made a face of disbelief. "Can you believe this creep?" she whispered. "Esme's got to see through him."

"She made the mistake of trusting him once before," Nancy reminded Bess, her voice low.

"We've got enough shots without the change of clothes," Janine announced, coming toward the dressing room. "Let's call it a day. I think it's time we went back to the hotel and you had a nice long sauna, Esme."

"That sounds like heaven," Esme said. Then she called Nancy and Bess over. "You girls are coming to the masquerade ball I'm hosting tonight at the hotel, aren't you?"

"You're kidding!" Bess said.

Nancy had heard Bess mention the ball, but it was by invitation only. Excited, Nancy realized it would be a chance to keep an eye on all the suspects—including Kim and Janine.

"But we don't have costumes," Bess pointed out.

"I wouldn't let that stop you," Esme said with a laugh. "Janine can give you the address of a costume shop where we all got ours. By the way, you have to come dressed as a character from one of my novels, so pick your costumes accordingly."

"That sounds like fun," Bess said. "Thanks for inviting us."

Janine led a weary Esme out of the studio with Todd following. Nancy waited to see if Giancarlo and Kim might appear, but they seemed to have left while Esme was talking to Todd. Nancy and Bess hailed a cab and headed back to the Barrington to pick up Nancy's car. Bess was eager to go straight to the costume shop, but since Nancy had to stop by the police department to turn the suitcase over to Sam, the girls split up. Bess caught a cab and would pick up two costumes. Nancy was free to drive over to the River Heights Police Department then.

Sam wasn't in, so Nancy left the evidence with the sergeant on duty, and also wrote a note to Sam about the latest incident, asking him to call when he got in. On the way home Nancy tried to make sense of what she knew so far. It was obvious that whoever was harassing Esme knew her well enough to know her old nickname. That person held enough of a grudge against Esme to want some serious revenge. Most of the harassment was centered around *Telling All*. The note writer had warned that if Esme went ahead with *Telling All,* her life would only get more miserable. The question then was, why would someone not want Esme to publish the book? Better yet, who would want to stop Esme from writing it?

One person came to mind right away: Todd Gilbert. He could have a lot to lose personally and professionally if the book painted him in a bad light. But would he go so far as to threaten Esme's life?

Meanwhile, Kim Scott had the means to put the spider in Esme's suitcase. There appeared to be more than a little tension between Kim and Esme, but was that enough for Kim to go after her boss? Or was she working with someone else, someone like Todd?

And then there was Janine. The publicist had access to the press room, and also had a key to Esme's hotel room. She might have gone up to the room and put the spider in Esme's suitcase.

By the time she pulled into her driveway, Nancy was so keyed up she didn't feel like sitting around and waiting for Sam to call. After saying hello to Hannah and pouring herself a glass of juice, Nancy sat down in her father's study and plotted her strategy. It wasn't too late to make some phone calls to New York. Nancy quickly put in a call to Janine at the Barrington, and five minutes later she had the numbers for Esme's publisher, editor, and agent in New York.

Conrad O'Brien, Esme's editor, was actually on his way to River Heights to attend the masquerade ball that evening, but his assistant was able to answer some of Nancy's questions. Apparently, along with the notes there had also been a series of phone calls made by someone using a voice disguiser. The caller warned that Esme's life would be in danger if she went ahead with the book. Susan Segal, Esme's agent, was able to give Nancy an even better lead. Although she hadn't gotten any phone calls, she had noticed that the notes began to arrive around the time that Kim Scott had called Susan, asking if she would represent her work.

"Kim is a writer?" Nancy asked, perplexed.

"Of course," Susan Segal told her. "That's why Kim went to work for Esme in the first place. Esme promised to help her with her career, but Esme didn't know that Kim wasn't very good. She's done what she can to help, but I think Kim holds it against her that she hasn't been able to do more."

Nancy thanked the woman, and after hanging up the phone, it rang almost immediately. It was Sam. "I hear there's a hot party at the Barrington tonight," he said.

Nancy laughed. "Who told you that?"

"Never mind," he said. "Since I'm invited and you're invited, how about going together?"

"As in a date?" Nancy asked.

"Well, actually, yes," Sam said.

Nancy was surprised to find herself blushing, and she was suddenly aware of what a nice voice Sam had: low and intense. "My friend Bess is going, too," Nancy reminded him.

"I'll pick you both up," Sam said. "I don't mind the company."

"I just got off the phone with Esme's agent." Nancy then proceeded to explain what she had learned from Susan Segal.

"It looks like we've got a solid lead there," Sam agreed. "Let's keep our eyes on Kim Scott."

"Did you get anywhere with the notes?" Nancy asked.

"I've scanned them all into our computers," Sam told her. "We've got some great new software that can analyze the threats to determine if they were all made by the same person. If so, the program can also give us a tentative make-up on that person."

"That's neat," Nancy said.

"The computer is running through the threats now," said Sam. "It should take until tomorrow morning before we have anything solid. Meanwhile, when and where should I pick you up?"

Nancy gave Sam her address and reminded him it was a costume ball. "I have just the thing," Sam told her. "See you at eight?"

"Sounds great," Nancy said.

As soon as she hung up, Nancy thought about Ned for an instant. Then she had a strange sensation, and she realized with a start what it was: guilt! She felt guilty about going to Esme's ball with Sam!

Nancy shook herself, throwing off the thought. It was nothing, just a party. Besides, Bess would be there.

So why was she already imagining her first

dance with Sam? Why did the thought send a warm glow through her from head to toe?

Esme's ball was in full swing by the time Nancy, Bess, and Sam arrived at nine. Bess had rented a beaded dress for herself, and a blue ballgown, glittering with rhinestones for Nancy. Bess was going to the ball as Billie Kasper, a heroine from Esme's 1920s historical novel set in New Orleans, *Jazz Nights*. Nancy's costume was meant to represent Jewel Trelawny, a feisty character from one of Esme's eighteenth-century historical romances. Sam was dressed in a dashing maroon velvet suit complete with a flowing white poet's shirt.

"This is going to be so much fun," Bess announced as they were about to enter the Barrington's elegant ballroom.

Nancy, Bess, and Sam stopped in the doorway to take in the transformation of the ballroom into a fantasy of romance and revelry. Panels of sheer gold fabric floated from the ceiling, creating diaphanous walls for the dancers to pass around and through. The partygoers were given handfuls of red, heart-shaped confetti to toss. Already it sparkled across the littered floor. The room was lit in soft blues and pinks, and everyone glowed and looked terrific in their romantic costumes. A big band played slow, romantic standards from a raised platform at the end of the room.

Nancy spotted Esme, resplendent in a flowing

white ballgown, dancing with Giancarlo, who wore a tuxedo. Todd, also dressed in a tux, whirled an elegant Helen Klein around the floor. A very Edwardian Bob Samuels came by, in high-waisted pants and a frock coat, to ask Bess to dance.

"How could I say no?" Bess asked.

As Bess whirled off on Bob's arm, Nancy spotted another woman across the room, dressed in her same costume. "Look," she said, pointing out the woman to Sam, "There are two of me!"

"I sincerely doubt there could be," Sam said gallantly. There was a slightly awkward pause, which he finally filled by asking, "Do you want to dance?"

"Sure," Nancy said. As Sam led her onto the floor, Nancy felt that same warm glow pass through her. Quit it, Drew, she told herself. You've got a guy already, and besides, Sam's older. He's not interested in you.

Or was he? When Sam took her in his arms, Nancy saw a half smile turn up the corners of his lips. Then he pressed her to him, and Nancy let herself get lost in the music, the moment, and the warmth of his arms around her.

Then she felt someone touch her hand and push a piece of paper between her fingers. Nancy saw Giancarlo whirl by, with Esme in his arms. Before she could say a word to him, they were gone.

She pulled away from Sam, who was surprised

to find Nancy ending their dance so abruptly. "Someone passed me this note," Nancy explained, unfolding the piece of paper.

When she read the note, Nancy's heart started beating faster, and she had to take a deep breath before she could read it out loud.

"'Only you know how much I care, cara mia. Please do not doubt my love. I promise, I swear —the future is ours! Yours, and yours only, G.C.'"

It was a love letter to her from Giancarlo!

Chapter

Six

ACROSS THE ROOM Giancarlo was having a conversation with the woman who was dressed like Nancy. With a start, Giancarlo saw Nancy glance his way.

"Kim!" Nancy said out loud. The woman dressed like her was *Kim,* and all at once Nancy realized that Giancarlo must have intended the note for Esme's assistant.

Sam figured it out as Nancy did. "Come on," he said. "We're going to ask that guy some questions. And they won't be in Italian!"

Giancarlo was standing alone by the time Nancy and Sam got to him. Esme was dancing with Bob Samuels, while Bess was gliding across the floor in the arms of Todd Gilbert.

"Cara!" Giancarlo cried when he saw Nancy.

"Did you get my note?" he whispered, his voice low.

"I certainly did," Nancy replied. "But I'm not convinced you meant me to have it."

"What?" Giancarlo blinked several times, and held his hand to his chest. "You doubt my affections? You think I would lie?"

"We think you got the wrong girl," Sam told him. "Our guess is you meant to give that note to Kim."

"You haven't shown a single bit of interest in me until just now," Nancy pointed out. "Kim is wearing exactly the same costume. Why would you pledge your undying love to me? Kim seems more likely."

Just then the song ended, giving Giancarlo an excuse not to answer. He peered past Nancy to the dance floor, and called out, "Esme! You promised me the next dance. Excuse me," he said, kissing Nancy's hand. "I thought you would be flattered at my note. Obviously, I was wrong. I give these notes to women sometimes, to keep their lives full of romance and longing, but I never meant for it to cause trouble—for me, or for you." Nancy took his speech to be a plea for her not to tell Esme.

"I understand," she said.

"*Grazie,*" said Giancarlo. With that, he strode onto the dance floor and took a radiant Esme in his arms.

"Bushwah," said Sam after Giancarlo was gone. Distractedly he ran his hands through his dark brown hair. "Or, as they say in the streets of Little Italy, baloney. The guy's a liar. He meant for Kim to have that note, and we all know it."

"I couldn't agree more," Nancy said, her eyes on Giancarlo. "What's going on between Kim and Giancarlo, and does Esme have any idea?"

"And does it have anything to do with the threats against Esme?" Sam finished.

Bess arrived, breathless from her dance with Todd. "It's hard to believe those things I've read about Todd and his temper," she announced. "As far as I'm concerned, Todd Gilbert's a dream."

"That's not what Esme thinks," Nancy said.

"I know, and he's really worried about that," Bess confided. "Todd's sure Esme's going to paint the most unflattering portrait of him and their time together. He's begged her not to, but she's adamant about telling the truth." Bess took a pad and pen from her evening bag and started scribbling madly.

"What are you doing?" Nancy asked.

"Taking notes," Bess said.

"For what?" asked Sam.

"For the romance novel I'm going to write," Bess told them. She scanned the room and wrote more. "Esme told me that if you're going to write, the best thing is to write from experience. So I'm writing down what I remember from the conversation I just had with Todd."

"When you're done with that," Sam told her, "Nancy's got some good material to add to your novel."

"Really?" Bess asked, her nose in her note-book.

"Giancarlo wrote me a love letter," Nancy announced and produced the paper.

Bess stopped writing to read it. "Wow!" she said, glancing up at Nancy with incredulity on her face. "This is unbelievable! Let me copy it down, okay?"

"We should give you the background, Bess," Sam told her, laughing lightly. "Don't you want to make sure you have the note in its proper context?"

Bess tapped her pen on her notebook. "You bet I do. Shoot."

Nancy explained her suspicions about Giancarlo's meaning to pass the note to Kim. Bess's eyes traveled the room, first to Giancarlo, who was standing with Esme by the refreshment table, and then to Kim, who was just disappearing through the huge wooden doors after giving a surreptitious glance in Giancarlo's direction.

"Where's she going?" Nancy wondered aloud, finishing with her story.

"I'll find out," Sam said. He took off along the perimeter of the room in pursuit of Kim.

"I can't believe this," said Bess, who by now had stopped writing and was simply standing with her mouth agape. "What you've told me is better than any romance novel."

"Let's get some punch," Nancy said. "I don't believe Giancarlo about giving lots of women these notes. I want to try pinning him down before the evening ends."

"What will you say?" Bess asked, following Nancy to the refreshment table.

"You're the budding novelist," Nancy joked. "What do you think I should say?"

Bess thought for a moment. "I know," she announced. "Call his bluff. Tell him you were suspicious before, but now you're ready to accept his everlasting love. Tell him that you can't live without him, that—"

Nancy hugged her friend. "I think that's enough, Bess. If it's okay with you, I'll play it a bit cooler."

"Suit yourself," Bess said loftily. "You asked for my advice and I gave it to you."

Giancarlo was no longer at the refreshment table, but Esme was still there, talking to a group of fans, including a tall, dark-haired man whom she introduced as her editor, Conrad O'Brien. Todd Gilbert was also there, and Nancy remembered that Todd had been cast to play Conrad in the screen version of *Telling All*. Conrad was younger than Nancy had imagined, and she could see a slight resemblance between him and Todd, especially if Todd wore horn-rimmed glasses like Conrad's. Nancy and Bess excused themselves to fill their punch glasses. The group around Esme slowly dispersed, until Todd and Esme were alone.

"Promise me you won't reveal our secret," the

actor pleaded. "That's all I ask. If you can make me that one promise, I'll stop bothering you."

"Oh, Todd," a weary Esme said. "Did you really think I'd reveal our secret? How would *I* look if the whole world knew the most intimate details of what went on between us?"

Todd took both Esme's hands in his and stared deeply into her eyes. "Do you really love Giancarlo? Is there really no chance for us?"

Esme withdrew her hands and turned away from Todd. Nancy and Bess found themselves behind a palm tree, no more than ten feet away from the romance writer. Esme didn't seem to notice them, however, and drew a tissue from the evening bag she was carrying to dab her eyes.

"No, there isn't," Esme said finally, her voice almost too low to hear. "At one point, I thought we could get back together, but it's too late. We can be friends, but that's all."

Todd pulled Esme close to his chest. The embrace went on until Janine's voice sounded through the crowded hall. "Before the evening is taken over by romance, I know Esme wants to share a few words with you. Esme?"

Todd released Esme, and Nancy saw that before Esme walked across the glittering dance floor toward the podium on the stage above the orchestra, she took a moment to compose herself. She touched up her lipstick and checked her makeup in the small compact she carried. A moment later, after a final squeeze of Todd's hand, she strode confidently toward the podium.

"Do you think she still loves him?" Bess asked, motioning in the direction of Todd. The actor followed Esme with eyes full of longing.

"I'm not sure," Nancy admitted. "But he really does seem hung up on her."

Giancarlo appeared onstage beside Esme. The couple posed, and the bright flashes of photographers' cameras filled the room for several minutes. Nancy found herself checking the door for some sign of Sam, wondering where he'd gone.

Suddenly a small backstage area to Esme's right began to fill with smoke. Janine's face registered surprise, but Esme had started speaking and clearly did not want to be interrupted.

"I want to thank you all for coming tonight," Esme said, not noticing the smoke. "It means so much to me to share my love of romance with others, to bring joy and pleasure into this sometimes gray world of ours."

The smoke was thicker now. Why was Esme continuing? Janine gave instructions to Giancarlo, who disappeared backstage.

"This isn't supposed to happen, is it?" Bess asked. "It's not a romantic effect or anything?"

"No," Nancy said. "That's real smoke, not dry ice."

Right then the red curtains erupted into flame.

The audience started screaming, and, after calling to Esme, Janine hustled her off the stage.

Esme didn't move fast enough. In the seconds it took for her to react, the fire moved from the curtains and onto her dress.

"Someone help her!" Nancy found herself crying. "Esme's on fire!"

Chapter

Seven

E SME!" TODD CRIED OUT, racing toward the stage. "I'll save you!"

The actor leapt onto the stage and wrapped his arms around Esme to beat out the flames.

Nancy, meanwhile, had also moved into action. While the frantic crowd screamed and pushed toward the exit, Nancy grabbed a fire extinguisher she spotted tucked into a corner beneath the stage. Then she climbed onto the stage and doused both Esme and Todd with blasts of foam. After that, she turned to the backstage area. Nancy didn't stop shooting foam from the extinguisher until she was sure that the fire was completely out.

Nancy quickly traced the fire to a huge box of Valentine's Day decorations stored beside the stage. Esme's name was written on the box, along with a note that they were to be used for a Valentine's Day bash to be held two evenings later.

After she was sure the fire was out, Nancy started to check the box of decorations to see if there was any evidence to indicate how the fire was set. But the smoke was still so thick that it filled the backstage area, making it difficult to breathe. She had to return to the stage to see how Todd and Esme were doing.

Soggy and wet, the actor and the romance writer stared at Nancy. "Whoever set that fire wanted to harm Esme," Todd warned.

"I'm just glad you reacted so quickly," Esme said. Todd offered Esme his arm. "Take me back to my room, please. This has been an awful day!"

Janine and Giancarlo came to the edge of the stage to look after Esme. While they all escorted Esme from the room, Nancy headed toward the backstage area. The smoke had cleared enough by now for her to investigate the box of decorations.

Careful not to disturb any evidence, Nancy used a nearby broom to stir the charred contents of the box. The air was thick with soot, and she coughed several times. After searching for several minutes, Nancy didn't find anything. She was about to give up when a small, matchbooklike object caught her attention. Leaning in closer, Nancy spotted what could have been an incendiary device like the ones arsonists used—the ashy remains of some material tied around a slow-burning match.

"Bingo," Nancy said aloud. "This fire was set intentionally."

"And I think I know who did it," a male voice added.

Nancy turned toward a winded Sam Fanelli, bent over and catching his breath. "I had the guy cornered in the parking lot, but he got away. Almost ran me down in his car, too!"

"What happened?" Nancy asked.

"I went to follow Kim," Sam said. "Well, she led me on a wild-goose chase into the basement. You'll never guess what's under this hotel. Anyway, I got as far as the gym—"

"The gym!" Nancy said. "She left the party to go work out?"

"You got it," Fanelli agreed. "But I lost her when she went into the women's locker room. So I waited on the gym floor, but she didn't show up. Finally, I decided to leave. On my way back here, I ran into some guy in a trench coat and a hat running as if there was no tomorrow. Naturally, I followed. He led me to the parking garage, but I lost him when he got into an elevator and took it to another level. Next thing I know, a car's coming at me so fast I had to dive to avoid it. Unfortunately, I didn't get the license plate. Sorry, kiddo. I don't want you to think you've got a lame partner."

"I don't!" Nancy protested, resisting the urge to give Sam more reassurance. "Can we be sure it was Kim?"

"We can't," said Sam. "But she did disappear right then, and I was following her. Kim's tall, and if she wore a trench coat and hat, I suppose she could pass for a man."

Nancy let out a deep sigh. "If we confronted her, I doubt she'd tell us the truth. We're just going to have to go on the suspicion that it could have been her." Then she called Sam over to show him the device she spotted. "What do you think?" she asked, pointing to the charred matchstick.

"I think we've got an arsonist," Sam agreed.

Terri, the hotel manager, came rushing backstage with firefighters in tow. The fire marshal agreed with Nancy's assessment of arson. Nancy and Sam spent the next half hour answering his questions. Finally, they were free to go. Bess had gone to check on Esme after her ordeal. She came back to the ballroom just as Nancy and Sam were finishing up with the fire marshall.

The three walked through the now deserted ballroom, kicking up clouds of heart-shaped confetti.

"It's so sad," Bess said, surveying the aftermath of Esme's masquerade ball. "Someone really is out to ruin Esme and destroy all the pleasure she gives to people. I hope we can stop this person, Nancy," she said.

"I hope so, too," Nancy said as they left.

After dropping Bess off at her house, Nancy and Sam parked in front of Nancy's house and discussed the case for a long time. Sam agreed it was time to run background checks on Kim, Todd, and Janine, since they were the prime suspects: Kim because of the spider incident and because she disappeared into the hotel's gym right before the fire was set. Todd because Nancy had the distinct impression that the actor couldn't be trusted. And Janine because she had the opportunity to ruin the press room. Meanwhile, Nancy agreed to stick close to Esme. Someone needed to be on the scene when and if the harassment continued.

"We make a good team," Sam said. "Between the two of us, we'll have this guy cornered in no time."

Nancy started to open the car door. "I'll call you tomorrow," she said.

"Hey, Nancy—" Sam began.

"What?" Nancy turned back to Sam and was utterly disarmed by the warmth of his brown eyes. His arm was over the back of her seat, and his hand lightly brushed her hair off her face.

"Nothing," he said. Then he coughed and let his hand fall. Nancy still had the sensation of his touch on her face, and she didn't want to admit to herself just how pleasant it was.

"See ya," she said, finding her voice.

That night Nancy lay in bed with all sorts of

confusing pictures in her head—of being in Sam's arms, of feeling his fingers in her hair and on her cheek, of what it would be like to kiss him.

But she stopped, forcing herself to remember that she had a boyfriend, that Sam was older, that he probably didn't like her anyway. That she'd never do anything to ruin things with Ned. At least she hoped she wouldn't.

Friday morning Nancy picked Bess up at ten and zoomed over to the local television studios where Esme was doing a taping for a talk show. As soon as she got in the car, Bess asked Nancy about Sam.

"You've been hanging around Esme too much," Nancy said. "There's nothing between us."

"Actually, I've got pretty good radar," Bess scolded Nancy. "For example, I can always tell when a guy likes a girl. And believe me, Sam likes you."

"Oh, Bess," Nancy protested, "He's several years older than I am, and besides, I'm in love with Ned."

"That doesn't stop you from having a crush on someone else," Bess said, her eyebrows raised. She picked at a stray piece of lint on her cream wool coat and retied the multicolored scarf that held her hair back. "Esme says scarves are romantic. What do you think?"

Eager to change the subject, Nancy reassured

her friend that she looked great, as usual. "Maybe you'll get on camera," she said.

"My thoughts exactly!" Bess announced. After they drove in silence for several minutes, Bess banged her head with the palm of her hand and said, "I can't believe I forgot to show you this." Bess handed over the front page of that day's *Today's Times*. Even as she drove, Nancy was able to see that one of the lead stories was by Brenda, reporting on Esme's press conference. When they came to a stop light, Nancy skimmed the article. What she found surprised her.

"Brenda included the story about the black widow," Nancy said. "But she wasn't there."

"She must have an inside source," Bess said.

"Like Janine Halpern, for example," Nancy concluded.

"Remember how chummy she was with Brenda at the press conference," said Bess. "What if Janine is Brenda's source? What if she's the one who called Brenda in the first place, and got her to come to the book signing and ask Esme all those questions?"

The light turned green and Nancy accelerated through the intersection. "I've thought about that. Janine doesn't mind the negative publicity, that's for sure. But was she the one to set the fire last night or put the spider in Esme's suitcase?"

Bess shivered. "She was close enough both times. If she did, she's no friend of Esme. We should warn her about Janine."

69

"We shouldn't warn Esme about anything," Nancy corrected Bess. "At least not until we're sure ourselves."

At the studio the taping was about to begin. The girls got as far as the entrance to the studio, where they saw Giancarlo. Esme's husband spotted Nancy and Bess and gave them both a hearty greeting.

"Nancy! Bess!" he exclaimed. "I'm so glad to see you!"

With that, Giancarlo fell upon Nancy's hand, putting it to his lips. "How can I ever thank you for not revealing our secret to Esme? Now that I know I can trust you, I want to tell you the truth. I was angry with Esme, very angry, for how she lost her temper with Kim earlier, and I wanted to make her jealous in return. She saw me passing the note to you, and it drove her mad! After the fire, we were able to settle our differences. She apologized to me and promised to apologize to Kim, too. So! You see what a favor you did us all."

Giancarlo kissed Nancy's hand, and then pecked her twice, once on each cheek. Nancy felt his whiskers brush her face, and saw, up close, how clear and blue his eyes really were.

"Thank you, *cara*. I'm sorry I could not tell you the whole truth last night."

"I understand," Nancy said, not at all sure that she did. Was Giancarlo telling her the truth now, or last night, or was the real story the one he wasn't telling: that he really had intended to pass the note to Kim? And why did Giancarlo care so much about the fact that Esme was rude to Kim in the first place?

Bess was scribbling away in her notepad, and only raised her eyes when Giancarlo opened the door to the studio and ushered them both inside. There, Esme was sitting, all glamour and radiance in a fitted black velvet dress with gold and red trim. Her trademark pearls were at her ears, and a triple strand of pearls dangled around her neck. Her rich, dark hair was pulled back in a fashionable chignon, revealing her long, graceful neck. Giancarlo went immediately to his wife, took her in his arms, and kissed her passionately, much to the delight of the audience and Emily Wells, the show's host.

"People, people," she cried over the sound of applause, "we're about to start. Let's keep it down until the cameras are rolling, okay?"

Nancy and Bess took seats next to Janine. As the publicist leaned forward to greet them, Nancy was surprised to see Brenda Carlton seated on the other side of Janine.

"Hi, Nancy," she said, waving smugly. "Hi, Bess!"

"Great," said Bess under her breath. "Who invited the world's biggest big mouth?"

"I have one guess," Nancy whispered into Bess's ear. "And I'm sitting right next to her."

The show started taping, and even Nancy found herself caught up in the excitement. Members of the audience stood and thanked Esme for the thrill and excitement her books had brought to their lives. One by one, Esme answered their questions: Yes, she tries to write as much as possible from direct experience. No, she never had a steamy affair with Prince Haroun. As for the rumor that she was once secretly married to the famous recluse Ted Stephens, Esme had only one reply. "You'll just have to buy my autobiography," she said, her green eyes sparkling mischievously, "and read about it there!"

After a short break Emily Wells began fielding phone calls on the air from their listening audience. Esme had taken two or three calls, all flattering and full of requests that Esme verify some bit of rumor or gossip. Then a caller came on the line whose voice sounded strange and distorted, and Nancy's ears pricked up. Unless she was wrong, the caller was using a voice disguiser.

"Admit it, Esme," the caller pressed, "you haven't really done all those things you claim. You've never been to Nepal or the Middle East. I'll bet you never even met Ted Stephens. In fact, I think everything about you is a lie."

"Hold on!" Emily Wells shouted, her face red with anger. "What right do you have to insult our guest like that?"

"Yeah, who are you?" an audience member cried out.

"I'm a friend," the caller announced in the same creepy electronic voice. "A friend of the Black Widow."

Both Nancy and Bess gasped. Their harasser was on the line! From the pallor of Esme's face, Nancy saw that the romance writer had come to the same conclusion.

"Why don't you tell us who you are?" Nancy cried out. "What kind of coward hides behind a mask?"

"I'll reveal myself soon enough," the caller said. Then, with a dull hum, the line went dead.

Chapter
Eight

THE TALK SHOW AUDIENCE reacted in an uproar. Emily Wells quickly cut to a commercial, while Esme, her face white and her hands trembling, fell into Giancarlo's arms. Beyond Janine, Brenda was furiously scribbling away. In frustration, Nancy realized that once again they were powerless to stop whoever was harassing Esme.

"Maybe the person will call back," Bess said hopefully.

"I doubt it," said Nancy.

By now, the show was back on the air. Emily Wells addressed the camera and spoke earnestly. "Harassment of the kind we just witnessed is terrible. If this is the price of Esme's fame, then it's a horrible price. I'm sure you all join me in wishing Esme only the best. Our thoughts are with you, Esme. We love you!"

The audience burst out in another round of applause. As the show wrapped up, Esme's smile was forced and strained. She stood with her arm around Giancarlo, waving to her loyal fans. "Thank you!" she cried. "Thank you for your support!"

As soon as the cameras stopped filming, Giancarlo led Esme out of the studio. Nancy didn't have a chance to go over what had just happened with the romance writer, but she could find Esme at the Barrington later if they needed to discuss the case. Meanwhile Nancy's careful eye noticed that Kim Scott was nowhere to be seen. Had Esme's assistant missed the taping entirely? Could she have made the call?

Janine was talking to Emily Wells. Since the publicist was busy, Brenda rushed over to Nancy instead, and started throwing questions at her.

"What do you know about that caller?" Brenda asked. "Is Esme being stalked? Is someone out to ruin her reputation or her career? Was that the same person who put the spider in Esme's suitcase?"

"How did you find out about that, Brenda?" Nancy asked, her eyes narrowing on the reporter.

Startled, Brenda's eyes flitted around the room. "I don't have to reveal my sources," she said defensively.

"But you do need to have more than one to verify a story," Bess reminded her. "I took a journalism class, too, you know."

"Did the same person who sent you to the

Barrington tell you about the spider?" Nancy asked.

"Maybe, maybe not," Brenda replied. She flipped her notebook shut and scowled. "I can see you two aren't going to be any help. I'll have to get my information somewhere else."

"Why don't you try that source of yours?" Bess called out as Brenda walked away. Once the reporter was gone, she made a face. "She makes me so mad. Do you think the person harassing Esme is actually tipping off Brenda?"

Nancy thought for a moment. "Possibly, except why would Brenda still have so many questions about that caller—unless the person harassing Esme is only tipping Brenda off partway. My guess is that Brenda knows less than we do; she's simply more careless with what she does know. Come on," Nancy went on, taking Bess's arm. "I've got to call Sam to tell him what happened."

In the lobby of the building, Nancy spotted Pia Wieland coming from the ladies room, wearing her customary eyeglasses and big straw hat. She walked toward them, frowning, and said, "What a terrible thing! Don't you just feel for Esme? Who could have done such a thing? Well, I must be going. See you girls later."

Nancy and Bess said goodbye to Pia. Then Nancy stepped over to the nearby bank of phones. She quickly dialed Sam's number.

"I'm hacking away, Nancy," he told her.

Sam had that wonderful low voice, Nancy thought. Why did it get to her so much?

"Did you come up with anything?" Nancy asked, shielding her expression from Bess's prying eyes.

"Something," Sam confirmed. "Although it wasn't what I expected."

"What?" Nancy asked, excited.

"Todd Gilbert's got a record," Sam told her. "For battery. And that's not all. Esme Moore once had a restraining order against him."

"You're kidding!" Nancy exclaimed.

"What is it?" Bess asked.

Nancy quickly told Bess what Sam had learned. Then she asked Sam, "Anything on the profile of our harasser?"

"Nothing yet," said Sam. "From what I can tell, this software has a million bugs in it. The first bio it gave me was for a middle-aged woman. You don't want to know the rest! But I'm going to run the notes through one more time. Hopefully we'll come up with something useful. Listen, I saw in the paper that Esme's giving a reading at the Barrington this afternoon. I thought I'd drop by. Maybe we can go out afterward to discuss the case?"

"Okay," Nancy said, blushing. Bess raised an eyebrow to question Nancy. Leave it to Bess to know exactly what was going on in Nancy's mind! Nancy hung up the phone and faced Bess's scrutiny.

"Well?" Bess asked. "What was that about?"

"Sam's coming by the Barrington this afternoon for Esme's reading," Nancy explained. "He wants to go out afterward to discuss the case."

"I see," said Bess. Her eyebrows arched another inch. "And what did you say?"

"You heard!" Nancy protested. "Honestly, Bess, you'd think I was going on a date with him or something."

"Isn't that what you'd call it?" Bess asked.

"No!" Nancy insisted. She shouldered her purse and folded her arms across her chest. "There's nothing between Sam and me. We're working on a case together, that's all."

"Okay, okay," Bess said. She held her hands out, palms up. "I'll back off. I don't need to remind you of Ned, or that tomorrow is Valentine's Day and that you should call him and work things out. I don't need to tell you that Sam's an older guy, and he's probably just playing with you."

By now Nancy's face was bright red. "I know you mean well, Bess, but it's not what you think. Really. Now can we get back to the case?"

"Sure," Bess agreed. But on the way over to the hotel, Nancy could tell that Bess was still preoccupied with Sam and the fact that Nancy had agreed to go out with him after Esme's reading. Nancy tried to talk to her friend about the latest developments in the case.

"I hope Esme is willing to talk to us about the restraining order she once took out against

Todd," Nancy said, pulling out of the parking lot. "Do you think that could be the secret Todd wants Esme to leave out of *Telling All?*"

"Could be," Bess said.

"I wonder, though. Is that enough to hurt Todd's chances of a comeback?" Nancy asked.

"Sure," Bess replied. She stared out the window at the passing scenery.

"Todd has the motive to harass Esme, but his behavior isn't as suspicious as other people's. For example, what about Kim?" Nancy said. "She could have put the spider in Esme's suitcase, and she wasn't in the audience during the taping just now. She could have made that call."

"Kim doesn't seem to like Esme very much," Bess agreed. "But what's her motive?"

Nancy reminded her friend about what Esme's agent had told her about Kim's writing career. "Kim may feel betrayed by Esme. She may think Esme isn't delivering on her promise to help her out."

"I suppose," Bess murmured, then said nothing for the remainder of their ride to the Barrington.

By the time they got to the hotel, Nancy had to say something. She gave her keys to the valet, and when she and Bess were standing on the curb, Nancy said, "I feel like you're mad at me, Bess, and I don't understand why. Is it because of Ned? Do you think I'm not being fair to him?"

"Listen, Nancy," said Bess. "I like Ned, but my problem is that I think you're not being honest with yourself. If you like Sam, then go for it. Stop pretending."

Nancy was torn. Should she tell Bess she *had* been thinking about Sam that way or should she wait until she understood better how she felt?

"This is crazy!" she said out loud. "I don't know how I feel, and you're making it harder. What if I did like Sam? Would that be so bad?"

Bess smiled a little. "No, but you'd have to tell Ned, wouldn't you?"

Nancy let out the deep breath she felt she'd been holding since she met Sam. "I know, Bess, I know."

"You're afraid to do that when nothing's really happened between you and Sam, right?" Bess asked.

"I guess so," Nancy admitted. "Does that make me a bad person?"

Bess hugged Nancy to her. "Of course not. You're just confused. Who wouldn't be? Sam's a great guy. You have a lot in common. He's new and different and you've been with Ned a long time. Maybe you need to let things take their course and see what happens."

"Is that okay?" Nancy asked. "I feel like I'm not being honest."

"You are," said Bess. "You're honestly confused!"

They both laughed. "I feel much better," Nancy said, taking a deep breath.

"Good," said Bess with a firm nod of her head. "Now let's get on with this case. Or else I'll think you're dragging it out just so you can be with Sam."

At Esme's suite, Janine answered the door. The publicist told Nancy and Bess that Esme was in the Jacuzzi, but that the two girls should join her there.

"She's at her most relaxed in the Jacuzzi," Janine said. "I'll find you some suits."

"Are you sure?" Nancy asked. "I don't want to disturb her, but I do have a few questions to ask."

Janine was already halfway toward the bedroom. "She won't mind, I'm positive." She returned with a pair of black swimsuits, two robes, and some towels. "Here you go. You can change in the locker room downstairs."

The health club was located in a basement floor below the lobby. Nancy and Bess changed in the locker room and headed toward the Jacuzzi. There Esme was alone, quietly relaxing in the bubbling water with her eyes closed. She looked up when Nancy and Bess entered the tiled room and seemed genuinely happy to see them.

"I live for these things," Esme said, floating in the water.

Nancy stepped into the hot water, sitting across from Esme. Bess settled in next to her. "We wanted to ask you a few questions," Nancy said. "Janine said you wouldn't mind if we came down here."

"Shoot," Esme said, her eyes closed.

Nancy gently explained what Sam had learned about the restraining order Esme had placed against Todd. "I know Todd is worried you'll reveal a secret of his in *Telling All*. Is that the secret Todd was mentioning?" Nancy asked.

"I'd rather not say," Esme told her, blotting her face with her towel.

"You did place a restraining order against him," Bess insisted.

"I did," Esme agreed. "But the reasons remain between Todd and myself. It's too personal."

"Is there some other secret Todd would want to protect?" Nancy pressed.

Esme opened her eyes and gave Nancy a firm look. "I'd really rather not say. Can we leave it at that?"

Nancy was momentarily distracted by several people walking past the glass door. Then she said to Esme, "I understand. But I need to know if you think Todd is capable of harming you to prevent the publication of *Telling All*."

"I honestly don't think so," Esme told her. "Todd may be headstrong, but he'd never do anything, not at this point, that would hurt his career. He must know that if he was caught, his chances would be gone completely."

Bess fanned herself and wiped the hot water from her face. "I don't see how you two can stand this heat," she said. "This water is way too hot. I'll meet you guys up in the room, if that's okay?"

Esme laughed. "It's an acquired taste, Bess."

As Bess stepped out of the Jacuzzi, Nancy was trying to think of the best way to ask Esme about Kim. She was about to speak when she became aware that Bess was pushing against the door in frustration.

"What's wrong?" Nancy asked her friend.

"I can't open the door," Bess said, her face beet red with the heat and the effort. "Nancy, help. We're locked in!"

Chapter

Nine

THAT CAN'T BE," Esme said, alarmed. "The doors don't lock."

Nancy rushed over to where Bess was standing. There wasn't any kind of lock on the door. Wiping the steam from the glass, Nancy immediately saw the problem. Outside, someone had slid a broom through the door handle, making it impossible to open the door from the inside.

"This water *is* too hot," said Esme, stepping out of the Jacuzzi, her body flushed.

"We're going to have to shout for help," Nancy said.

"I'm feeling faint," Esme said.

"Help! Someone help us!" She sat down on the ledge between the Jacuzzi and the door.

More steam rose from the water. The heat in the room continued to build as Nancy, Bess, and

Esme shouted for help. It was clear to Nancy that Esme's pursuer had struck again. After a minute the door flew open, and they all fell through the opening and into Janine Halpern's arms.

"What on earth!" Janine said. "I got a call from someone who claimed to have locked you in the Jacuzzi."

Esme drew deep lungfuls of fresh air and asked Janine for a glass of water. While Janine filled up a paper cup at a nearby water fountain, Nancy could see the strain this was causing in Esme. She was doing her best to hold up under the most difficult circumstances.

"Did you recognize the voice of the person who called?" Esme asked her publicist after drinking all her water.

"No," Janine said. "But I'm fairly certain it was the same person who called the television studio earlier today. At least, the voice had that same strange electronic quality to it."

Esme visibly sagged at the news. Her lips trembled, and she clutched the robe Janine had helped her into. "Why is this happening to me?" she said, a slight edge to her voice. "Who did I hurt so desperately that I deserve such revenge?"

"Easy, easy," said Janine, and put a comforting arm around her writer. "I know Nancy will find the person, and no one will remember any of this a year from now. Meanwhile, you need to get ready for the reading. Let's go back to the room. We'll order lunch, and I'll make you a cup of tea."

Esme sighed and turned her attention to Nancy and Bess. Nancy could see the dark circles under Esme's eyes. The romance writer gripped both girls' hands and said, "Won't you have lunch with us? It's the least I can do for you."

Bess grinned and impulsively reached out to give Esme a hug. "We'd love to, right, Nan? We can grab our stuff and change upstairs."

"Sure," said Nancy. "Give me a second, though. I want to ask a few people if they saw anyone near this door."

"We'll wait for you by the elevators," Janine said.

Nancy made a quick tour of the women's locker room while Bess retrieved their clothes and went to join Janine and Esme. Nancy asked several people if they'd seen anyone around the Jacuzzi; most gave Nancy an apologetic smile. But the last woman she asked told Nancy that she'd been heading to the pool from the locker room when she saw a tall person wearing a trench coat and hat standing by the Jacuzzi door. Pressed, the woman couldn't give Nancy a better description, but Nancy already knew more than she had started with: whoever had locked them in the room fit the description of the person Sam had chased the night before.

Nancy hurried to the elevators. Bess handed her a robe, then shot her an expectant look. "I think we've got a suspect," Nancy told Bess, Janine, and Esme. In the elevator ride up to

Esme's suite, Nancy shared her news with the three women.

"That sounds like the same person who set the fire last night," Bess exclaimed.

Nancy agreed, slipping into her tennis shoes. "I'll call hotel security and tell them to keep their eyes out for someone fitting this description. In the meantime, we have to figure out how this person always knows where Esme will be, and when."

Inside her robe, Esme shivered. "This is just too creepy."

The elevator opened on Esme's floor. Nancy was the first to get off, and when she started down the hall, what she saw surprised her. At the end of the hall, someone was letting himself out of Esme's suite, someone with a pile of papers in his hand. That someone was wearing a trench coat and hat!

"Stop!" Nancy cried. "Don't move!"

The tall, trench-coated figure hesitated for a moment. The person was wearing sunglasses and leather gloves, and it was impossible for Nancy to get a good look at the face. When she called out, the figure took off at a run, and Nancy raced after him. Turning a corner, she just saw the person step into another elevator. As the doors closed, a paper fell to the floor. Nancy scooped it up and quickly scanned it. The thief had stolen Esme's manuscript of *Telling All!*

By now, Esme, Janine, and Bess had caught up

with Nancy, who was frantically waiting for the second elevator in this bank to arrive.

"It was our man," Nancy announced. "He stole Esme's manuscript!"

The other elevator arrived just as Esme fell to the floor in a dead faint. "We'll take care of her," Bess told Nancy. "You go after the guy!"

Nancy guessed that the thief wouldn't bother to get off at another floor, but would travel all the way to the lobby—the easiest route out of the hotel. When her elevator reached the lobby, Nancy had her suspicions confirmed. She spotted the retreating figure of her suspect weaving his way through the crowd. At the hotel's revolving doors, the person stopped to see if he was being followed. Catching sight of Nancy, the suspect quickly pushed his way through the doors and out onto the street.

Ignoring the stares of hotel guests, who were surprised to see a woman in a bathrobe and sneakers race through the lobby, Nancy took off at a run. At the front entrance, the suspect was dashing across the hotel's circular driveway toward the street.

"Stop that man!" Nancy cried.

The suspect turned, saw Nancy, and dropped several more pages of Esme's manuscript, which went flying away in the wind. Nancy darted between parked cars and chased the suspect onto the busy city street.

"You're not getting away from me this time,"

Nancy said through gritted teeth as she pursued the thief up the street.

She was no more than fifty feet behind her quarry, weaving around noontime pedestrians. Nancy felt herself getting closer. A stoplight at the end of the block turned yellow, then red, and Nancy had to wait a moment to make sure a car in the cross traffic didn't hit her. In that moment's hesitation, Nancy saw Esme's harasser hail a cab.

"No!" Nancy cried, but it was too late. The yellow taxi squealed to a halt, and, with a last glance over the shoulder at Nancy, the suspect got into the waiting cab. By the time Nancy darted between the passing cars, the cab was gone.

Burning with adrenaline and frustration, Nancy tried hailing a cab herself. One after another, yellow taxis passed her by. Then she realized: she was wearing a bathrobe! No one would pick her up dressed like that. Dejected, Nancy turned and headed back to the hotel. There, a bellhop closely scrutinized Nancy as she passed through the bronze and glass revolving doors.

"Don't ask," she said, shaking her head ruefully. "You don't want to know."

Bess was waiting for her in the lobby. "What happened?" she asked.

"I lost the guy," Nancy said in exasperation. "He took off in a cab."

"Esme's pretty upset," Bess said to Nancy as

they made their way toward the elevators. "She's got other copies of *Telling All,* but that one had all her notes and revisions on it. She'll have to redo all her work."

"I was so close," Nancy said, getting into an elevator.

Bess reassured her friend. "Don't worry, Nan," she said. She pushed the button for Esme's floor and the doors closed. "I have a feeling that wasn't the last time we'll see that person. You'll get another chance."

Inside the suite, Nancy saw that Giancarlo and Janine were having a rough time trying to calm a distraught Esme. "We will find this person," Giancarlo was saying. "We will get the manuscript back!"

"It's not that simple," said Esme, the tears in her eyes ready to spill over. "Don't you see? This person isn't going to stop at stealing my manuscript. Whoever it is wants to ruin me entirely!"

"Cara—" Giancarlo tried to take Esme in his arms, but she threw him off.

"You're no help!" she cried. "Where were you when this happened? You're useless except for a photo opportunity. I should just drop you right now!"

Nancy coughed uncomfortably. "I'm afraid I lost our suspect," she said, trying to break the tension in the room.

Esme, clearly embarrassed at the sight of Nancy and Bess and by what they'd just overheard, immediately composed herself. "We think," she said, "that whoever stole the manuscript was the same person who called Janine to tell her we were locked in the sauna."

"That's likely," said Nancy. "The theft was clearly planned. But we need to find out how that person got into this room."

Nancy quickly got on the phone to Terri, the Barrington's manager. After letting her know about the theft, and learning that there were no missing keys to Esme's suite, Nancy hung up. "They're going to change the locks, but it seems to me that this person must have an inside track at the hotel. How else could he get into Esme's room not once, but twice?"

"You mean the spider," Bess guessed. "You think the person has a pass key?"

"Could be," said Nancy. "Still, after Esme's reading, I want to do a little legwork to see if Terri or anyone else has any idea how this person keeps getting into Esme's suite."

Janine ordered club sandwiches for the girls, a big tossed salad for Esme, and iced tea all around. Nancy hadn't realized how hungry she was, but after they changed back into their street clothes, both she and Bess wolfed down their lunches. When they were done, Janine prepared a pot of Esme's special herb tea, and the girls went downstairs to wait for Esme's reading to begin. There, in an intimate parlor off the hotel's main lobby, Brenda Carlton greeted Nancy and Bess with a hearty hello.

"I got a tip that Esme's reading is going to have

a surprise ending," Brenda told them, her face open and eager.

"From your source?" Bess asked.

"None other," Brenda agreed.

"Won't you give us a hint who your source is?" Nancy asked. "That person may be able to help us figure out who's been harassing Esme."

"Why should I help you?" Brenda asked, arching her dark eyebrows. With that, she walked toward the front of the room and took a first-row seat.

Just then Nancy spotted Kim entering the room. "Now where has she been all this time?" Nancy wondered aloud.

"Janine said Kim has been feeling sick today," Bess explained. "I guess she's feeling well enough to come down for the reading."

In Kim's hands was a large manila envelope, and she was studying its contents. Bess went to choose seats, and Nancy casually walked over to the assistant. As Nancy approached, Kim stuffed the sheaf of papers into the envelope and clasped it shut. Nancy's heart skipped a beat. Kim had a manuscript in that envelope. Was it the stolen copy of *Telling All?*

Nancy was about to question her when she heard someone call out her name. She turned to see Sam Fanelli waving to her as he approached. Kim used that moment to sneak away.

"How's it going?" Sam asked. "Any news?"

Nancy told Sam about getting locked in the

Jacuzzi, the theft of the manuscript, and how she'd chased the suspect. Then she shared with him her suspicions about what Kim might have in the envelope she held. The whole time Sam stood close to Nancy and listened intently. Nancy tried not to think about his warm brown eyes and the way his longish hair curled at his collar.

"Do you think Kim's the suspect you chased?" Sam asked.

"Could be. Would she fit the profile of our harasser?" Nancy countered.

"I'm still waiting on that program," Sam said ruefully.

By now the room was filling with guests. Pia was sitting inconspicuously at the back of the room. Nancy spotted Bess beckoning to her from the seats she was holding. Esme entered, along with Giancarlo and Janine.

"I guess we should take our seats," she said quietly.

"I'll sit with you," Sam said. "We can go over all this stuff after the reading is over."

Like a true friend, Bess had saved two seats for Nancy. She shot her friend a knowing look as Nancy and Sam sat down and Esme moved to the front of the room. "Watch out, Drew," Bess whispered. "Esme's stuff can be pretty romantic."

Nancy blushed and was keenly aware of Sam's hand draped lightly across the back of her seat. He wasn't exactly putting his arm around her, but he was definitely moving in that direction, and Nancy found herself a little uncomfortable —and maybe a little excited.

The crowd hushed. Esme took a sip from the teacup she'd brought with her. "I'm going to read a section from *Passion*," she said. "I hope you enjoy it." Without further introduction, Esme flipped through the book she held and started reading. As the woman's husky voice filled the room, Nancy sneaked a peek at Bess, who had her eyes closed and was obviously drifting off into Esme's romantic universe. As the writer went on, Nancy, too, found herself escaping into Esme's story. A young woman, caught in a dangerous country, hiked through enemy territory with the man sent to rescue her. Each night they camped out beside a romantic fire, and each day they passed through beautiful but treacherous countryside. As the tension built, Nancy became all too conscious of Sam's proximity, his hand on the back of her chair, the fact that his fingers could so easily reach out to touch her hair.

In the midst of this reverie, Nancy became aware that Esme was having difficulty reading. The writer was constantly interrupting herself to cough and sip tea and clear her throat, until finally she held her hand to her neck, obviously choking.

Then, right in front of her audience, Esme fell to the floor, unconscious.

Chapter

Ten

C ALL AN AMBULANCE!" Giancarlo shouted, rushing to Esme's side. *"Cara mia!"* he cried, taking Esme into his arms.

Janine scrambled up from her seat and ran out of the room to summon aid. Nancy and Sam jumped up and went to help Giancarlo, but there was nothing they could do. There was some slight movement behind Esme's closed eyes, but otherwise the writer remained unconscious.

When Esme had fainted, the room fell silent. Now, slowly, audience members began whispering among themselves. Nancy saw Pia in her seat in the back straining to see over the crowd. When Nancy spotted Brenda heading quietly toward the door, she knew immediately that this attack would be in Saturday's paper.

Meanwhile, Sam had positioned himself beside the small table where Esme had put her cup of tea. He leaned close for a whiff of the beverage. Instantly, Nancy understood what he suspected.

"Poison?" she whispered, moving to stand beside him.

"Very possibly," said Sam. "That was an awfully sudden fainting spell."

The paramedics had arrived and were gingerly lifting Esme onto a stretcher. Janine answered questions from two police officers who had arrived with the paramedic crew.

Bess came over to Nancy and Sam. "I'm going to the hospital with Esme," she said. Looking over her shoulder at the emergency workers, she wrung her hands at the sight of Esme, laid out flat on a stretcher, being wheeled from the room. "Unless you need me here?"

"Go ahead," said Nancy. "When Esme comes around, I'm sure she'll want to see a few familiar faces. I'll meet you there later."

Bess took off after the paramedics, and the two police officers came over to question Sam and Nancy. Sam identified himself, then explained his suspicions about Esme's tea.

"We'll get the evidence team down here," said one officer.

"We need to find out who made the tea," said Nancy. "If it was Esme or Janine. The tea bags are probably in her room, so we should make sure to get that evidence, too."

"Good," said Sam. "If she was poisoned, the

hospital should be able to give us a toxicology report from blood tests. Call them and be sure they know to look for poison."

"Will do," the second officer said, nodding her head.

"Let's check out Esme's room," said Sam. "These guys can take care of things downstairs."

Nancy and Sam were crossing the lobby when Nancy spotted Kim heading for the main brass and glass doors. "That's strange," she said out loud. "I thought for sure Kim would have gone with Esme."

Sam frowned at the sight of Kim standing in front of the Barrington. "Unless she doesn't care what happens to Esme," he said.

Nancy watched as Kim got into an old-style cab with a distinctive yellow-and-black checkerboard pattern on its door. "Maybe she's going to the hospital now."

"Or maybe not. Maybe where she's going has something to do with that manuscript you saw her holding. Come on," Sam urged. "I've got my car parked out front."

Nancy raced across the driveway to the street to Sam's compact. Nancy kept her eye on the cab Kim had taken, and gave directions to Sam as he pulled out into the afternoon traffic.

"There they are," she said, pointing to the cab, half a dozen cars in front of them. "I can tell you right now they're not headed in the direction of the hospital. We're traveling north. River Heights Memorial is south of here."

"Why am I not surprised?" Sam said, giving Nancy a wide grin.

Nancy tried to ignore the warm feeling his smile sent through her. "Do you think Kim is Esme's harasser?" she asked.

"The circumstantial evidence is there," Sam agreed. He weaved the car in and out of traffic, and Nancy had to hold on to the dashboard to prevent herself from sliding across the seat—and into his lap. "Is she our trench-coated culprit?" he asked rhetorically. "She's tall enough. The guy in the trench coat could actually be a woman."

"Where'd you learn to drive?" Nancy asked as Sam cut off yet another driver and got an earful of horn in response.

"Noo Yawk," Sam said, thickening his accent. He cut around a corner, still in pursuit of the cab. By now, they were only two cars behind it. Since the side street they were cruising on was quiet, Sam hung back a bit. At the end of the block, the cab driver stopped in front of a copy shop and Kim went in. Sam parked his car several hundred feet back. Ten minutes later Kim emerged from the shop and got back into her cab.

"What's she doing?" Sam asked, gripping the steering wheel and staring ahead intently. "Are we just following her while she runs her errands?"

"You're impatient, aren't you?" Nancy asked. "You of all people should realize how time-consuming detective work can be."

"I do," said Sam. "But it doesn't stop me from

being impatient. That's why we make a good team. You're cool as a cucumber, while I'm Mr. Antsy." They were at a stoplight and Sam glanced over at Nancy. "Am I right, or am I right?" he asked, the gaze from his chocolate brown eyes intense.

Behind them, a car honked. "The light's green," Nancy said, trying to ignore the effect he had on her.

Kim's next stop was the post office. By now even Nancy was getting frustrated, but she persuaded Sam that following her was still worthwhile. Kim was their only solid suspect. Finally, their perseverance paid off. On her last stop, Kim got out of the cab in front of an office building. This time, she paid the cab driver, who took off with a squeal of tires.

"See?" said Sam. "Even that guy was losing patience with all these errands!"

Nancy waited for Kim to enter the building. "I'll be right back, Sam," she said, getting out of his car. Then she followed, a short distance behind Kim. Inside, what Nancy discovered surprised her. Among the lawyers and accountants, the building also had a literary agent among its tenants. Nancy went back outside to report the information to Sam.

"You don't think she's trying to sell a copy of *Telling All,* do you?"

"I don't know," said Nancy. "But I say we confront her when she comes out."

For half an hour Nancy and Sam waited. They

chatted, and Nancy laughed at the stories of Sam's boyhood growing up in New York City in a section called Little Italy. It became easier and easier for her to talk to Sam—about detective work, about what it was like to be in dangerous situations, about traveling and how much they both liked that part of the job. Nancy kept having a nagging thought, though—I shouldn't be having this much fun with another guy. What about Ned? The next day was Valentine's Day. Should she call Ned, or would he call her? Would she tell him about Sam? There wasn't anything to tell, she insisted to herself, even as she enjoyed looking at Sam's brown eyes, his strong hands, his broad shoulders.

"Earth to Nancy!" Sam was saying, his hand cupping his mouth. "Suspect in sight. Will Detective Drew please come back to this planet?"

Nancy looked out the window to see Kim emerging from the office building. The manuscript was still in her hands, and there was a dejected expression on her face.

"Let's do it!" Sam cried.

Kim was more than a little surprised to see Sam and Nancy coming toward her. "Hey," she said, "what brings you two down here?"

"Actually, we followed you," Nancy said.

Kim's mouth set in a straight line as she pushed her dark hair back from her face. "Oh, really?" she asked. She clutched the envelope she carried and held it to her chest defensively. "Why is that?"

"We have reason to suspect you've got Esme's manuscript there," Sam said, "and that you were trying to sell it to an agent just now."

Kim's eyes went wide. "You've got to be kidding!" She stared at Sam and then at Nancy. "You think I'm the person harassing Esme, don't you."

"You are a suspect, yes," Nancy confirmed.

Kim ripped open the envelope and shoved the manuscript at Nancy, who read the title aloud: *"Love and Folly,* a novel, by Kim Scott."

Nancy handed the sheaf of papers to Sam. "This is your own manuscript," she said to Kim.

"Disappointed?" Kim said, her hand on her hip. "You bet that's my novel. I was trying to sell an agent on it just now, but he wouldn't bite. What makes you think I could actually pass off *Telling All* as my own book anyway? Even in this town, every agent would recognize that as Esme's life story, not mine. I may not be crazy about Esme Moore and we may have our differences, but I would never harass her or anyone else for that matter. That's not a denial, that's the truth!"

Kim yanked her manuscript from Sam's hands and, pushing past the two of them, took off down the street at a fast clip.

"Phew!" said Sam, reeling a bit from Kim's outburst.

"I'd say Kim has had a hard time being in Esme's shadow," said Nancy. "Still, she's right about never being able to pass off Esme's manuscript as her own. I guess we should have thought of that."

Sam rubbed his stomach. "I'm getting too hungry to think straight. How about dinner?"

"Sure," Nancy said brightly.

"I know just the place," said Sam.

Ten minutes later Sam was pulling up to a small restaurant in one of the quieter parts of town. Inside red- and white-checkered table-cloths and red candles cast a warm glow and atmosphere. Garlic, bread, and tomato sauce filled the air with their pungent aromas. Nancy's stomach growled and she suddenly realized just how hungry she was.

They were seated at a corner table with a view of the street, and after ordering they slathered butter onto thick slices of warm, yeasty bread.

As they ate they discussed the case. Sam still thought that Kim was a viable suspect, but Nancy disagreed. "I know she has the motive and the opportunity," Nancy said. "But somehow I get the feeling that Kim really wouldn't harm Esme. Where would it get her?"

"Revenge," said Sam, digging into his spaghetti. "Many cases of harassment come down to that, anyway."

"What's going on with your computer program, by the way?" Nancy asked. She cut off a bite of lasagna and blew on it. "You haven't mentioned it lately."

"That's because the thing stinks," Sam said. He sipped at his iced tea and smiled at Nancy over the rim of his glass. "If you could come up with one that worked, you'd make a mint, but this program isn't worth the paper it was requisitioned on."

"No luck?" Nancy asked.

"It keeps telling me I've got a semiretired woman between the ages of fifty and fifty-five. I keep telling it to try again."

"Maybe we should believe it," Nancy suggested.

Sam shook his head. "Nope. It doesn't make sense. My guess is we're looking at Kim or Todd. Not some part-time librarian!"

"What about Janine?" Nancy offered. She explained to Sam her suspicions that Janine might be giving Brenda information, and that the publicist didn't mind the negative press coming from all the harassment. Plus, she had had access to the press room.

Sam considered Nancy's suggestion. He leaned back in his chair and tossed his napkin onto the table. "It's an idea," he agreed. "You really do have a good mind for this, Nan. Ever consider a full-time career as a detective?"

Hearing Sam call her by her nickname sent another flutter through Nancy's stomach. "Maybe," she said, smiling.

Over Nancy's protests, Sam paid the check, then drove them both back to the Barrington so that Nancy could pick up her car. "This was fun," he said when they were parked. "We'll have to do it again sometime."

"Sure," said Nancy. She didn't want to sound too excited, or else Sam might get the wrong idea. And what might that be, Drew? a voice in her head asked as the valet drove up with Nancy's car. That you're interested?

On the way home Nancy remembered she had to meet Bess at the hospital. It was already eight o'clock, and visiting hours were probably ending, but Nancy thought it was worth it to swing by to see if Bess was still there and needed a ride home.

When Nancy got to Esme's room, the door was open. She went inside. A dim light was on, and the room was empty except for Esme. Just as Nancy entered, the phone rang on a nightstand beside Esme. The romance writer turned in her sleep, but didn't wake up enough to answer it. Nancy reached for the receiver, picked it up, and said, "Hello."

"Hello, this is Helen Klein. Who's this?" When Nancy identified herself, Helen asked to speak with Esme. Nancy told her the woman was asleep.

"I see," Helen said, pausing. "When she wakes up, could you have her call me? It's rather urgent."

"Is there a message I can pass along?" Nancy asked politely.

"No—that is—well, yes. Tell her I have some bad news," Helen said finally. "I hate to do this to her, but Bob has decided she's too controversial right now."

"I'm sorry?" Nancy asked. "Maybe you'd better explain."

"After everything that's happened, and now the poisoning . . ." Helen broke off, but finally blurted out, "Just tell her we can't go through with the movie project. The deal's off."

Chapter

Eleven

"Nancy," Esme murmured, opening her eyes. "What is it? I thought I heard the phone ring."

Helen Klein was in the midst of saying goodbye to Nancy, but the line went dead before Nancy could put Esme on the phone.

"That was Helen," Nancy said.

"Was she calling to find out how I am?" Esme asked weakly. The writer tried to sit up, but Nancy could tell from her pale face that even the slightest movement was an effort.

"Take it easy," Nancy said. "Let me help."

Nancy had just propped Esme up when Bess came into the room, her arms full of magazines and newspapers. "Hi, Nan!" she said brightly. "Where were you all this time?"

"I'll tell you about it later," said Nancy. "Right now, I'm afraid I have some bad news."

"What else could go wrong today?" asked Esme.

As gently as she could, Nancy broke the news to Esme from Helen. It took a moment for Esme to understand what Nancy was telling her, but as soon as the news sunk in, tears came to her eyes and she pounded the mattress with her fist.

"My entire career is in the process of being ruined!" she exclaimed. "Everything I have worked to achieve during the past ten years is slowly being eaten away by this person. What on earth did I do to deserve this? When will it end?"

Esme's tears began to flow and her body was racked with sobs. Nancy wondered how Bess would handle having her idol break down in front of her. At first, when Esme started crying, Bess was distraught, but a moment later she was sitting by her on the bed, handing her a box of tissues and trying to offer what little reassurance she could.

"I'm sure you'll get another movie deal," Bess said.

"Am I interrupting?" a voice asked. Todd Gilbert stood in the doorway with a huge, blooming poinsettia plant in his arms.

"I know how much you like them," he told Esme, entering the room. "Do you realize how hard a poinsettia is to find after Christmas?"

Esme took the plant from him and put it on the nightstand beside her bed. "Thank you," she said, drying her tears. "It's beautiful."

107

"I was so worried about you," Todd said. "When Janine told me—"

"I would have thought you'd be happy," said Esme. "If I were dead, I wouldn't be able to reveal your secrets, would I?"

By now Bess had gotten up from her perch on Esme's bed. "We'll leave you two alone," Bess said. With that, Nancy and Bess left the room, quietly closing the door behind them.

"Those two never stop, do they?" Nancy asked, shaking her head.

"It's a sure sign that they still really care about each other," said Bess. "I almost believe Todd when he says he was worried. Esme could have died."

Nancy remembered what Helen Klein had said about Esme being poisoned, and she asked Bess what she knew about it.

"They pumped Esme's stomach as soon as she got here," said Bess. "I guess they did a preliminary test and found out it definitely was poison. Tomorrow morning we're supposed to know exactly what kind of poison it was. They think it was some kind of plant."

"Esme's tea!" Nancy announced. "That's got to be how it happened."

Bess stifled a yawn. "I'm sure you're right, Nancy, but truthfully, I'm so tired right now I can't even think about it. What a day!"

"You're not kidding," Nancy agreed. She knew there wasn't much they could do until the next day, when the toxicology report came in. "Let's say goodbye to Esme and head for home."

Nancy poked her head into Esme's room, only to see Todd perched on the side of the writer's bed, her hands clasped in his and a searching look on his face, while Esme kept her eyes, teary now, downcast. Luckily, neither Todd nor Esme saw Nancy, who immediately drew back and whispered to Bess, "I don't get it. I thought Esme couldn't stand the sight of Todd, but she's letting him hold her hand."

"You're kidding!" Bess said, her blue eyes wide with wonder. "What's that all about?"

Nancy shook her head. "I don't know, but I have a feeling there's a lot Esme's not telling about Todd. She never really wanted to go into the details of the restraining order she placed against him, for example."

"What if Todd's behind the harassment and Esme's unwilling to let herself see the truth?" Bess said, biting on her lip.

"That just might make sense," Nancy agreed. "Let's hope that whoever turns out to be the harasser, Esme's prepared to accept the truth."

The next day Bess had promised to help her parents with chores and errands, so Nancy was on her own until the Valentine's Day Ball that evening. After breakfast Nancy checked in at the hospital and learned that the romance writer had left for the Barrington that morning. Unfortunately, Nancy couldn't get any details out of the hospital lab about Esme's poisoning. Remembering that Sam was planning to be in the office that day, Nancy called him at work.

"Just the woman I want to see!" Sam announced when he got on the line. "Come on over, I've got some news."

"Did your software program come through finally?" Nancy asked with a laugh.

"Nah," said Sam. "I'm sending that thing back to the manufacturer. It's a dud! Something much more interesting, but you'll have to come down if you want to know."

"I'm on my way!" said Nancy. She changed into a denim shirt to go with her jeans, and ran a brush through her hair. At the last minute, Nancy applied a coat of Fabulous Grape lip gloss that Bess had given her. Taking a final look before heading downstairs, Nancy saw she looked pretty good.

For a teenager, she thought. And Sam's not interested in any teenagers!

As she was putting on her jacket, the doorbell rang. A delivery person was standing on the porch with a huge bouquet of flowers.

"Nancy Drew?" the man asked.

"Yes," she said.

"Sign here."

Nancy signed the delivery form and took the flowers. As soon as she went back inside, Nancy felt a wave of guilt pass over her.

The flowers were from Ned. A card attached to

110

them read, "I hate to argue. You know how much I love you, and I'd never do anything to blow it between us. Call me. Love, Ned."

"Oh, Ned," Nancy said out loud. "I wish all it took were a few flowers!"

Immediately, she felt lousy about her reaction. But the truth was, even though she did miss Ned, and even though she did feel like calling him, she was also looking forward to seeing Sam. Hadn't Bess said that it was okay to be confused? Well then, she was confused, and the flowers from Ned hadn't helped matters at all. Nancy tried calling Ned at his fraternity house, but he was in the library working on his paper. She left a message and headed out the door.

At the River Heights Police Department, Sam was sitting behind his desk when Nancy entered the small, cramped room that was his office.

"It used to be a closet," Sam confirmed, his eyes lighting up at the sight of Nancy. He gestured to the folding chair beside the desk. "Have a seat," he said. "I can't wait to tell you what I found out."

"Esme was poisoned," Nancy said, jumping the gun.

Sam's chocolate brown eyes rested on Nancy's face. "How'd you know?"

"I stopped by the hospital," Nancy said. "Bess told me."

"The hospital lab called me this morning," Sam confirmed. "Poinsettia leaves, with spearmint to mask the flavor."

111

"Poinsettia," Nancy said, softly repeating the word. "Todd Gilbert visited Esme last night. He brought her a poinsettia plant. You don't think he'd be stupid enough—"

"To poison her with a plant and then bring her the same plant as a get-well gift?" Sam finished for her. He shook his head. "I doubt it. Probably just a coincidence."

"Todd said something about poinsettias being Esme's favorite plant," Nancy remembered. "Other people must know that, too. Could someone have poisoned Esme with the plant as some kind of weird joke?"

Sam leaned back in his chair and studied Nancy, who found herself blushing at the attention. "It's just an idea," said Nancy.

"It's a good one," said Sam. "I still maintain that Esme's harasser is someone who knows her well and harbors a grudge against her."

"So far, we know that could include Kim, or maybe even Todd, if he's worried about her revealing his secret." Nancy paused. "You know, there's someone we haven't even considered."

"Giancarlo," Sam said matter of factly.

"Yes," said Nancy. "He knows about Esme's nickname." Nancy remembered Giancarlo's excuse to her about the love note he gave her. "He could be angry at Esme for not caring enough about him. I've seen them fight, and it's not a pretty sight. Kim once said that Esme didn't love either Todd or Giancarlo. Perhaps Giancarlo is harassing Esme because he suspects she doesn't love him."

"Weird," Sam said with a shrug. "Why not just leave?" He turned to his computer. "I'll run a check on his social security file," he said. "Maybe something will turn up."

While the computer began its search, the screen went blank. Since there wasn't anything to watch, Nancy found her eyes being drawn to Sam, who, much to her embarrassment, was also looking at her.

"Listen," he began. "When this case ends—"

"Which we can only hope will be soon," Nancy said, casting her eyes down at Sam's desk. "I'm not sure how long Esme can hold out."

"I'm not worried about Esme," said Sam. "What I wanted to know was—"

A beep from the computer and a flash of white onto the screen told them that the information they'd requested on Giancarlo had come through. "Thanks," said Sam, turning in his seat to see Giancarlo's record on the screen. "Perfect timing!"

Nancy stared past Sam to the computer screen. Sam quickly skimmed the record and shook his head.

"Sorry, there's nothing here," he said. "The guy is in the country legally and doesn't have any kind of record—either here or in Italy. He's clean."

Nancy stepped behind Sam's desk to look at

the file more carefully. As she leaned in, her elbow accidentally brushed against Sam's cheek. "It is cramped in here, isn't it?" she asked, laughing nervously.

"You socked me!" Sam said, holding his cheek in mock pain. "I'll make you pay for that, Drew!"

"I'm sure you will," Nancy said, countering his banter. Then she skimmed the computer screen. Something in Giancarlo's vital statistics surprised her. "It says here Giancarlo is single. How old are these files?"

"They're supposed to be up to date," he said. "Why?"

"Esme and Giancarlo have been married for four years. Don't you think his social security file would reflect that?" Nancy asked.

"It should," said Sam, squinting in confusion. "Let's check something." Sam typed in Esme's name; a minute or two later, the romance writer's information came on the screen.

"According to her record," said Nancy, "Esme's single, too."

"I'll check the IRS records," said Sam. "I just happen to have a crucial password that will let me into their files—so long as I use it for research, and not illegal gain."

Sam hacked away at the computer. A few moments later Nancy and Sam were staring at both Giancarlo and Esme's IRS records. As far as Nancy could tell, the evidence was irrefutable.

"Both Giancarlo and Esme have filed single returns for the past three years," Nancy said, stunned at the information. "But that means . . ."

Sam finished for her. "The romantic fairy-tale couple who've charmed the world from River Heights to Rome, Italy, aren't married at all."

Chapter

Twelve

For some reason, then, Giancarlo and Esme have been lying about being married. Why?"

A thought occurred to Nancy, one she hesitated to suggest because it made Esme seem terribly cold and calculating. "Maybe the whole relationship is a publicity stunt," she said, thinking out loud as she went. "I remember Esme threatening Giancarlo with the words, 'I should just drop you right now.' Not, 'I should break up with you,' but 'I should drop you.' It didn't occur to me until just now, but doesn't that sound like someone breaking a contract?"

Sam nodded slowly. Then he grabbed his leather jacket from off a hook on the back of his door. "That's exactly what we're going to find out," he said. "Come on."

"Where are we going?" Nancy asked.

"To question Ms. Esme Moore herself," Sam replied, reaching across his desk to pull Nancy out from behind it. "And if this kid from Little Italy has his way, we're going to get some answers."

At the Barrington, Esme herself answered the door to her suite. Pale and wearing glasses, the romance writer looked a lot less glamorous and a lot more down to earth. Nancy thought that Bess might be disappointed to see her idol looking so plain without her glowing makeup and fabulous clothes and jewelry, but for Nancy, Esme's casual attire made it easier to ask the questions she wanted answered.

"Are we interrupting?" Nancy asked politely.

"Not at all," said Esme. "I was working, but it's nothing I can't put down. Come on in. What can I do for you?"

Nancy introduced Sam. "He's been handling the police side of our investigation," she explained.

"Pleased to meet you," said Esme, shaking Sam's hand.

"Esme, Sam and I have some questions to ask you," Nancy said. She sat down on the sofa while Esme took a seat in an armchair across from her.

Sam joined Nancy on the couch. "This may not be pleasant," Sam warned. "Occasionally the truth isn't."

Esme swallowed visibly.

Nancy leaned forward, her elbows resting on

her knees. Looking up at Esme, she plunged in. "Sam and I have reason to suspect that you and Giancarlo aren't married. Is that true?"

Esme sat back in her chair, shock expressed on her face. For a moment her glance darted back and forth between Nancy and Sam. She tried to speak several times, but simply ended up taking a succession of deep breaths. Finally she said, "It's true. I won't deny it. My agent and my publisher and I—I accept responsibility—all thought the pretend marriage would be an excellent publicity move." Esme smiled softly. "We've done nothing illegal, and there's never been any danger of our falling in love. And being 'married' to Giancarlo has helped my sales. However, you must know what a scandal you'll cause if this information gets past this room."

Nancy assured Esme that she wouldn't tell. "We're not interested in harming your career," she said. "We simply need to know who has solid motives for harassing you."

"Not Giancarlo!" Esme protested. "Of course, he has a contract with me, and I pay him dearly to be my traveling companion. But he and I both know that he can cancel at any time. He'd never use threats and tactics to break off the arrangement."

"What about Kim?" asked Sam. "She seems to have a big-time grudge against you."

Esme shook her head and stared at the floor. "I don't think so. Kim may seem tough and cool on the surface, but she'd never sink this low. And I do think she'll make it someday as a writer. She simply needs to be patient."

"Todd?" Nancy put in.

"I don't seem to be surrounded by the most trustworthy people," Esme said on a sigh. "Is that what you're telling me? Next, you'll be suggesting Janine."

Nancy held back from confirming Esme's suspicions. "Let's get back to Todd," she insisted gently. "Would he have reason to threaten you?"

"You were right," said Esme, wiping a tear from her eye. "This isn't very pleasant." The romance writer got up, crossed the room to the desk, and returned with a tissue to dab at her eyes. After blowing her nose, Esme went on. "Todd and I had an extremely volatile relationship. We loved each other madly, and sometimes that meant we also fought terribly. He's worried I'll write about all that. In fact, I did get a restraining order against him, but it's not what you think. He once threatened to kidnap a beloved cat I owned. I wanted to do everything I could to keep him away from poor Sophie."

Nancy exchanged a look with Sam. "That's the secret Todd is afraid you'll reveal?"

Esme smiled softly. "I know it doesn't seem like much, but imagine the press. 'Todd Gilbert threatened to kidnap prized cat.' It wouldn't look very good, would it?"

"Would Todd try to hurt you now?" Sam asked.

"I honestly don't think so," said Esme sadly.

"I've assured him I will never write about his threats, or the danger I felt I was in when we were together. The truth is, he never did harm me—or Sophie—and I do believe now that he has learned to control his anger. It's unfortunate, since the Todd I see now is someone I truly could love, if only there weren't such a past between us and the present weren't so complicated."

The room was silent. Nancy believed Esme, and thought how sad it was that someone who had devoted her life to romance and passion had seemed to miss out on the great love of her life.

"Is there anyone else?" Sam asked. "Someone from your past, from when you still lived here in River Heights maybe?"

Esme thought, her eyes closed. "I just can't think of anyone," she said.

Suddenly Nancy had a thought. "What if we read through *Telling All?*" she suggested. "If the harasser is someone from your past, we might find something in the book."

Esme nodded in agreement. "That's an excellent idea. Obviously, I don't have a perspective anymore on what's going on. My publisher sent me two copies after the manuscript was stolen. I'll get you one." Esme got up, went into the bedroom, and came out with a manuscript. "Needless to say, this is confidential."

"We'll keep it to ourselves," Sam said, taking the manuscript from Esme. "Let's hope your hunch is right, Nan, and we find our harasser somewhere in these pages."

After leaving Esme, Nancy and Sam stopped to pick up lunch. "We'll need a comfortable spot to read through Esme's book," Sam said as they were pulling out of a fast-food drive-through. "I don't feel like staying in the office all day. How about my place?"

Nancy took a long sip of the soda in her lap. "Sure," she said, trying not to act nervous.

Quit it, Drew, Nancy thought. He doesn't have anything in mind besides reading Esme's book and cracking this case.

Nancy couldn't relax. She remembered the huge bouquet from Ned. Yet here she was, driving through River Heights on a sunny February day—Valentine's Day—thinking about what Sam had planned for them when they got comfortable in his apartment. What was she doing? Nancy resolved that this thing with Sam had gotten out of hand. She was thinking about him too much. As soon as she got home, she'd try calling Ned again, tell him how much she missed him, make a plan to visit.

Sam's apartment was located in a quiet, residential area just west of downtown. He parked in front of a one-story, yellow-and-white cottage and quickly strode up the walk. Nancy followed him inside, where she found a cozy, one-bedroom apartment with hardwood floors and lots of light.

"Come on back," Sam called out.

In the kitchen, Sam was laying out their lunch on a scarred antique table. It was almost two, and Nancy realized she was starving. Esme's manuscript lay off to the side. Beyond the kitchen was a comfortable sun-room that looked out onto a small backyard. The room had a couch, several armchairs, and a stereo system.

"Nice place," she said, sitting down at the table and digging into her burger and fries. She and Sam ate in silence. When they were done, Sam cleared away the wrappers and headed for the sun-room, Esme's manuscript in hand.

"Why don't you take the first half, and I'll take the second," said Nancy.

Sam joined her on the couch, stretching his legs onto the coffee table. "I can see you like to be the boss," he said, handing over a thick sheaf of manuscript pages. "Let's race."

Nancy nestled back into a corner of the sofa and plunged into Esme's autobiography. Within a minute she was deeply involved in the story of how Esme had come to write her novel before *Passion,* and the experiences leading up to it. Apparently, Esme had been on a cruise, sailing around the world, and each night the captain of her boat told the guests of his adventures in China, the South Seas, Hawaii, and the Philippines. After the cruise ended, Esme stayed on board, sailing around the world once again to hear more of the captain's stories. These adventures became the basis of *Island Desires,* Esme's third novel to hit the best-seller list, and the one that made her name a household world.

"Having fun?" Sam asked. By now he was

stretched out along most of the couch. If Nancy moved her legs, she'd be sure to touch him.

"Learn anything?" he asked, sitting up.

"If you count how to become a romance novelist, then yes," Nancy said. "How about you?"

"I'm still in college with Esme," Sam joked.

After another ten minutes or so, Nancy noticed Sam was looking at her again. "Is something wrong?"

"No," he said, stammering. "I mean, well—kind of." Sam swallowed and turned on the couch so that he faced Nancy. Suddenly Nancy realized that Sam was holding her hand. "Nancy, I know this seems fast and everything, but I really—"

"Sam," Nancy said, her heart beating a mile a minute. "There's something I have to tell you."

The look in Sam's eyes was one of confusion. He held on to her hand, then leaned close enough so that Nancy could see the flecks of green in his brown eyes. "Don't talk," he said. An instant later, Sam's hand was touching her face, and then his lips were on hers. She held her breath, and the moment seemed to last forever.

"Wow," said Sam.

I'm in trouble now, Nancy thought, feeling Sam's lips brush her cheek, find their way into her hair, nuzzle her neck.

Nancy pulled back. It was awful to break the spell, and a part of her wished the kiss could go on and on, but she couldn't shake the thought of

Ned, and how she should tell Sam about him. "I'm seeing someone . . ."

"It's okay," Sam said. He let Nancy's hand drop after a final caress. "I understand. You don't have to explain. It's just that we work so well together."

"We do," said Nancy. "That's the problem." She got up from the couch and began pacing the room. "I'm so confused. I've been with Ned— he's my boyfriend—for a long time and I really love him. But spending time with you has been fun and exciting and—"

"And you didn't mind that kiss just now," Sam said.

"No," Nancy admitted, still feeling Sam's lips on hers. "I didn't."

"Listen," said Sam. "It's my fault. I rushed things. My mother always says I'm too impatient. I think you're great, Nancy. I'm not going to pretend I'm not interested. But I won't put any pressure on you, except to say that Ned sounds like a lucky guy and I hope he appreciates you."

"He does," Nancy said, thinking of Ned for what felt like the millionth time that day.

Sam sighed deeply and picked Esme's manuscript up from the coffee table where he'd set it down. "All this romance must be driving me off the deep end," he said, smiling ruefully. "Can we get any work done after that stupid move of mine?"

Nancy laughed and tried to quell the last remaining butterflies in her stomach. "Let's hope so. We've got a whole book to read."

Ten minutes later Nancy felt Sam poking at her leg. "Sam!" she cried.

"Sorry!" Sam said. "I think I found something. Check it out." Sam handed Nancy two pages from Esme's manuscript. "The passage that starts at the bottom—there."

Nancy began to read a paragraph that described Esme's first novel. "The book was called *Black Widow*. That was Esme's nickname."

"Read on," Sam urged. "Read about the plot."

Skimming the passage, Nancy was stunned at what she saw. "It says here that in the novel a character gets poisoned by her best friend."

"And what do they find out caused the poisoning?" Sam asked.

Nancy let the paper fall to her lap. "Poinsettia leaves."

Chapter
Thirteen

W EIRD, HUH?" Sam asked Nancy. "Unless I'm wrong, we may be dealing with some kind of copy-cat crime here."

Nancy thought for a moment. "That could be, but what I find more interesting is that someone knew about the details of Esme's first novel." Something nagged at her, and as she reread the pages she figured out what it was. "Hold on! It says here that the novel was never published. But she wrote it with a partner in River Heights." A name jumped off the page at her. "Pia Wieland!" Nancy practically shouted. Nancy explained who Pia was, and how she'd been at the first press conference, and the TV taping. "And at Esme's reading!"

Sam took the sheet from Nancy. "We're definitely onto something here," he said. "According to this, Pia's got to be over fifty."

"So?" Nancy asked, perplexed.

"Remember how my software kept giving us the profile of an older woman?" Sam asked.

"You thought it was bombing out," Nancy said, thinking quickly. "But maybe it wasn't. Maybe Esme really is being harassed by a middle-aged woman. Pia Wieland! Where's your phone?" she asked.

"In the kitchen." Sam followed Nancy into the kitchen. Within a minute, Nancy was on the phone with Esme, asking her about Pia.

"It's so strange that I didn't remember Pia," Esme said. "I wrote that part of the book a while ago, so the details weren't fresh in my mind. Besides, it's been ten years since I saw her."

"Why would Pia have a reason to hold a grudge against you?" Nancy asked. "A reason to seek revenge?"

"Pia and I met in a writers' workshop," Esme said. "We worked together for a year, but our collaboration didn't work out. I understand that she never succeeded on her own. We didn't keep in touch after we parted. Why would she do this now?"

"I'm not sure," said Nancy. "We're going to follow this lead. I'll let you know what turns up."

Nancy hung up with Esme and related their conversation to Sam. "This is a hot lead," said Sam. "I'll get an address on Pia and we can check it out."

By the time Nancy and Sam left Sam's apartment, the light was fading from the clear February sky. It was only four-thirty, but it would soon be completely dark. Nancy realized then that they didn't have much time before Esme's ball. In all the excitement, she'd completely forgotten about the party, which was scheduled to begin at six with cocktails, and then continue on through the night with dinner and dancing.

"I hope Pia's the one," said Nancy, watching the sun fade from the sky. "Wouldn't it be great if we could walk into Esme's Valentine's Day ball with the news that we've caught her attacker?"

"It would," Sam agreed. "But let's not count on it. We still need to find evidence to prove our hunch."

On their way across town, Nancy's excitement grew. She had a feeling Pia was the one; all the pieces were starting to fall into place. Pia must have harbored a grudge against Esme, one that she had nursed for many years. Now, she was enacting her revenge. The questions were: Why now? Where would it end? And could Nancy and Sam stop her before she struck again?

Ten minutes later Sam was pulling up in front of a nondescript two-story house with faded blue paint peeling in places. The driveway was empty and the lights were out inside.

"Good," said Sam, cutting the ignition. "No one's home to keep us company." He leaned back in the seat, obviously settling in for a wait.

"Let's go in," Nancy said. She opened the car

door and was about to get out when Sam put his hand on her shoulder and drew her back inside.

"Is that how you do it, Drew?" he asked, grinning.

"A lot of the time there's an open door or window. That's not breaking and entering," Nancy explained. "That's letting yourself in and waiting for the owner to return so you can speak to her."

"I see," said Sam. He seemed to consider Nancy's reasoning for a moment. Then he clicked open his own door and said, "If anyone asks, I wasn't here, I didn't see anything, and I don't even know you."

"Right," said Nancy. And that wasn't a kiss you gave me earlier, either, she thought, wobbly in the knees from the memory. She'd call Ned as soon as she got home and confess to him everything about Sam, including the kiss. Well, maybe not the kiss, but everything else.

At the back of the house Nancy found a door that opened to her touch. "Bingo," she said. "Come on in."

"I shouldn't be doing this," Sam said, stepping inside. "I really shouldn't be doing this."

"I won't tell," Nancy said. She pushed him through the door and followed.

They were standing in a laundry area. Through the open door, Nancy saw a kitchen, then the living room beyond. Moving carefully through Pia's dark house, Nancy quickly found the bedroom.

"I'll look in here," she said to Sam, who stood in the doorway between the living room and the kitchen. "You take the living room."

"Giving orders again, I see," Sam said with a smile. He saluted, and said, "Yes, ma'am."

"And don't disturb any evidence," Nancy warned him with a smile. "But I guess I don't have to tell you that."

"You must be used to working with amateurs," Sam joked. "I've got one question for you, Drew."

"Shoot—" said Nancy.

"If you do this so often, why haven't *you* gone to jail?" asked Sam.

Nancy smiled and shrugged. "Just lucky, I guess." Then she went into the bedroom to begin her search.

Half an hour later Nancy had discovered a trove of evidence against Pia. First, she found file boxes in the closet that were full of clippings about Esme—nothing too incriminating there, Nancy thought, except you had to wonder why someone would collect enough information about the romance writer to put together a biography of the woman. Next, Nancy saw a man's trench coat hanging in the closet. Then, behind the file box, she spotted a dying poinsettia plant with half its leaves cut off. Beside the plant was a book titled *Deadly Doses: The Amateur's Guide to Poisons*. That's when Nancy called out to Sam.

"I think you should come in here," Nancy

cried out. Using a handkerchief to pick up the book, Nancy noticed a bookmark at a page describing poinsettias, along with a list of other necessary ingredients. "Check it out," Nancy said to Sam when he came into the half-dark room.

Sam took the book from her. After scanning the page and the list, he let out a low whistle. "The toxicology report says the poinsettia leaves were masked with spearmint. And here it is, right on Pia's list: spearmint leaves." Holding the book with his left hand, Sam handed a slip of paper to Nancy with his right.

"It's a receipt from a specialty pet store," Nancy said, barely able to make out the writing.

"For a black widow spider," Sam informed her. "What do you think of that?"

"I think we've got enough evidence here to put Pia away for a long time," Nancy said.

"I don't need to remind you that first we'll need a legal search warrant," Sam replied in a mock serious tone.

"I know that," Nancy replied, feeling a bit defensive. "I guess you could really get in trouble for being here," she said. "I'm sorry."

"Hey," said Sam, "I accept full responsibility. Besides, I wouldn't be the first guy to lose his head over a girl, would I?"

"I guess not." Even in the dark, Nancy could feel herself blushing. Alone in Pia's dark house and excited at the thought of cracking the case, Nancy found herself wishing her life wasn't so complicated and that she hadn't put off Sam so strongly back at his place. But the sound of a key in the front door quickly snapped Nancy out of her reverie.

"Pia!" Sam announced, peeking out the bedroom window to the street. "Quick, hide!"

Before Nancy could react, Sam was scuttling under Pia's bed. Nancy realized it was the safest hiding place and found she had no choice but to follow. A moment later her nose was full of dust, Sam's elbow was poking into her side, and Pia's ankles were visible as the woman walked into the bedroom and headed for a closet. Nancy could hear her rummaging around, and then detected what sounded like the chamber of a revolver being spun around, checked, and then clicked into place.

She's got a gun! Nancy wanted to shout to Sam. They couldn't be sure, but if Nancy was right, Esme's life could be in serious danger.

Pia walked toward the door again, stopping momentarily by the bed. Now her feet were facing Nancy, and Nancy saw Pia was wearing what looked like men's shoes and cuffed pants. The whole time, Pia had been dressing like a man to put Nancy and Sam off her track. That was why she wore the trench coat, the man's hat. The planning that had gone into Pia's revenge sent a chill through Nancy, made worse by the fact that Pia was standing next to the bed. If she discovered that Nancy and Sam were hiding right by her feet . . .

Pia didn't find them, though. A moment later she left the bedroom, and Nancy heard the sound of the front door closing. She waited five seconds, then crawled out from under the bed and raced to the window. There Pia was getting into a late-model sedan. Sam was out from under the bed by now and beside Nancy at the window.

"She's going after Esme, I just know it!" Nancy cried. "We've got to stop her."

Chapter
Fourteen

PIA WAS PULLING AWAY from the curb. Urgently, Nancy held on to Sam's arm and dragged him from the room. "We've got to follow her. I'm sure she's going to the Barrington. Pia's got to know about Esme's ball tonight. What better way to get to Esme, finally, than to ruin her ultimate party?"

Sam was looking out the front door now, careful not to be seen by Pia. "She's at the end of the block," he told her. "Come on. Let's go!"

Nancy followed Sam at a run out to his car. Sam had the engine started before Nancy was even inside. "You *are* impatient," she said with a smile as she slammed the door. "Just be sure you're not so eager that Pia knows we're behind her."

"Please," said Sam, peeling away from the curb

with a squeal of rubber. "I've got a bit of experience, as you know."

"I figured," said Nancy, her excitement rising. The chase was on! She was sitting in the passenger seat for once, able to enjoy the ride. Maybe she could get used to having an equal for a partner. Maybe it was a good thing—or a great thing—that she and Sam worked well together. If that were true, then maybe it would also be better not to be involved, to keep their relationship professional.

"Earth to Nancy," Sam said. "Beam in, Nancy." He held his hand to his mouth as if it were a microphone. "Suspect is in sight. Detective is out to lunch."

"Sorry." Nancy laughed. "It's so unlike me to have my mind wander like this."

"I think I understand," said Sam, taking a hard turn that made Nancy lean into him. Both of Sam's hands remained steady on the steering wheel, but Nancy could remember what it felt like to be touched by him. "Everything will work out," Sam reassured her. "Maybe this is one situation you can't think your way through. Maybe you'll just have to let your heart lead you."

"Telling me not to think is like telling me not to breathe," Nancy said, laughing. "Look out. Pia's taking that left."

The light went from green to yellow as Sam swung through it, his tires squealing and his shocks bouncing. "You know where we're going, don't you?" Sam asked.

Nancy nodded. "I have a pretty good idea." The sun had set and the streetlights were on as they headed from Pia's neighborhood toward downtown. Nancy looked at her watch. "It's six o'clock. Esme's ball should be starting any minute."

"True," said Sam. "So what's her plan?"

Nancy shivered, her eyes riveted to Pia's late-model sedan a few cars ahead of them. "I hate to think. Whatever it is, I'm sure Esme's in danger."

Pia led them through the busy downtown streets, until they were just a few blocks from the Barrington. In fact, the hotel was in sight when Pia went through a light as it changed from yellow to red. Sam had to screech to a stop at the light, while Pia cruised through.

"Rats!" Sam said, pounding the steering wheel. "Now she's got a head-start on us. What if we lose her?"

"We won't," said Nancy. She knew Pia would head for Esme's room. From there, she didn't know exactly what to expect. As she waited for the light to turn green again, Nancy bit on a fingernail, trying not to imagine the worst.

Sam inched out into traffic. The crosstown light was just turning yellow, and Nancy could see Sam resisting the urge to go through the red light.

"Go!" Nancy shouted as soon as the light turned green.

Pia was long gone. Sam raced toward the

Barrington's front entrance and threw the keys at the valet.

Inside, they raced for the elevators and caught a glimpse of Pia as the doors to one elevator closed.

"There she is!" Nancy cried out. "I knew it. She's headed for Esme's room. Come on!"

Another elevator appeared, and Nancy pushed her way onto it. To her dismay, the elevator proceeded to stop at every floor to let someone either on or off, and it felt like forever before she and Sam reached Esme's floor.

"Talk about impatient," Sam whispered, his eyes on Nancy's tapping foot.

"We could have walked faster," Nancy whispered back.

Finally they were getting off on the sixth floor. Nancy raced down the hall toward Esme's suite. What she saw there made her stop dead.

Pia had Esme in her grip. The romance writer was dressed in a full-length red gown, ready for her ball. The expression in her green eyes was one of pure terror. In a flash, Nancy realized why: Pia had a silver-barreled gun and was holding it at Esme's side.

"Nancy!" Esme cried when she spotted her. "Help me, please!"

Pia's face contorted into an expression of anger and frustration. "No one's going to help you this time," she spat at Esme. "Can't you see that you're going to have to come clean, finally?"

"I don't know what you mean," Esme said. She struggled to break free of Pia's grip, but the woman was strong. She held Esme more tightly, sticking the gun deeper into Esme's side. "What are you planning to do?"

"You'll see," said Pia. "Nothing more than you deserve—Black Widow."

Pia's voice as she pronounced Esme's nickname dropped to a mean whisper that sent shivers down Nancy's spine. It was obvious that Pia's desire for revenge was enough to make her take desperate measures. They had to stop her!

Giving Sam a meaningful look, Nancy took a small step forward. At the same time Sam called out, "Pia, let's talk. Let's be reasonable. If you harm Esme, you'll be in serious trouble. Why don't you reconsider?"

Slowly, while Sam distracted Pia, Nancy tried moving forward. The expression in Esme's eyes was desperate, yet hopeful. But Nancy hadn't taken more than three steps before she heard an explosion and saw a flash.

"Nancy!" Sam cried. "Get down! Pia's shooting!"

Nancy fell to the carpet, face first, her heart pounding. That was too close, she thought. She didn't look up until Sam was by her side.

"That woman is nuts," he said. "Are you okay?"

"I'm fine. Where'd she go?" Nancy asked, getting to her knees.

"As soon as she shot at you, Pia dragged Esme to the fire stairs," Sam told her.

A second later Nancy was racing toward the fire exit with Sam by her side. Once they were in the stairwell, Nancy could hear the sound of Pia and Esme, a few flights down. Nancy flew down the stairs, taking them three at a time. But as soon as Pia realized Nancy and Sam were after her, she started shooting up the stairwell.

Nancy pressed herself against the wall. "I guess she wants us to keep our distance," she joked, panting.

"I think you're right," Sam told her. "Let's stay close enough to follow her. As soon as we get downstairs, I'll call for backup. It looks like we'll be needing some."

After reaching the bottom of the stairwell, Pia led them down a series of corridors. Soon they were passing by the Barrington's enormous kitchen, heading for the banquet rooms. Keeping a safe distance behind, Nancy and Sam trailed Pia and a still-struggling Esme all the way to the ballroom.

"She knows these hallways like the back of her hand," Sam said, running beside Nancy.

"I have a feeling that Pia must have worked here," Nancy replied, catching her breath. "She probably stole a pass key at some point."

"I bet you're right. That must be how she got into Esme's suite," Sam said.

Now, Pia was pushing Esme through a door.

"Hurry!" Nancy cried, following them. Nancy yanked the door open to discover that they were standing in the backstage area of the Barrington's ornate ballroom. From behind the stage, Nancy could hear the crowd murmuring and the strains of the orchestra as it played the evening's first songs.

Sam was beside Nancy. They both hung back in the shadows, while Pia dragged Esme to the front of the stage.

"What's she doing?" Sam asked.

"I'm afraid to find out," said Nancy.

With one hand, Pia was pawing at the curtains to pull them open. With the other, she held the gun pointed at Esme's side. Nancy knew that if they were going to disarm Pia, now was the time. Quickly, Nancy assessed the situation. She'd need to sneak up on the woman, and the only way to do that would be from the side. Or, Nancy thought, noticing a catwalk above the stage, from above. A ladder went from the catwalk to the floor. Beside the ladder was a long rope. Nancy could climb the ladder, haul herself onto the catwalk, tie the rope to the catwalk, and use it to swing onto Pia from above.

Nancy whispered the plan to Sam. "That sounds dangerous," Sam said.

"We don't have any choice," said Nancy. "If we try to tackle Pia from both sides, she might shoot Esme."

"You're right," said Sam. "I'll cover her on the ground. Be careful."

Hitching the rope over her shoulder, Nancy began her ascent. Below, she saw that Pia had the curtains open. From the crowd came a murmur of surprise, and Nancy spotted Bess in the audience. When Bess saw Nancy, she put a hand to her mouth and clutched the arm of the man standing next to her. Other members of the audience spotted Nancy, too.

No! Nancy thought. By now, she was on the catwalk, frantically tying the rope to the railing. If Pia noticed the audience staring up at Nancy, then the plan was foiled. Keep your eyes off me! Nancy thought, shaking her head slowly at the crowd.

Bess and the others must have gotten the message, because an instant later the whole group had turned their attention to Pia and Esme.

"Can I have your attention," Pia was saying. "My dear old friend Esme Moore has an important announcement to make."

While Pia pushed Esme closer to the crowd, Nancy grabbed the loose end of the rope and quickly fashioned a loop to give her a handhold. She moved as fast as she could, but her fingers were jittery.

Now is not the time for nerves, Drew. Just do it!

"She wants to tell you all about her very first novel," Pia went on, her tone mean and spiteful. "The one she supposedly wrote all by herself."

Nancy had lowered herself to the catwalk's

floor and was about to slip over the edge. Below, she caught a last glimpse of Sam's encouraging gaze. Then she shifted her gaze to Pia. What she saw made her stomach turn in fear.

The woman was staring up at Nancy. "Stop right there!" Pia cried. "Or else I'll shoot."

Chapter

Fifteen

Unfortunately it was too late for Nancy to change her mind. She was already balanced to fall off the catwalk, and that's exactly what she did, closing her eyes and swinging off it, praying that Pia wouldn't be able to focus on her.

"Nancy!" Bess shouted.

"Look out!" Sam cried.

Daring to open her eyes, Nancy saw she was flying right toward Pia's arm. She readied herself to kick out. If her timing was right, maybe she could jar the gun from Pia's hand.

"Esme!" Nancy cried. "Duck!"

As she swung toward Pia, Nancy lashed out with her leg. Pia pulled Esme to the floor with her, and while Nancy was looping out over the stage, Pia used the opportunity to drag Esme off toward an exit.

"Stop them!" Nancy called to Sam. "They're getting away!"

Sam was already in motion. Nancy let herself drop from the rope onto the stage. She joined Sam, who had taken three long strides across the stage and was hot on Pia's trail. They were on the opposite side of the stage from where they'd come in, and Pia seemed to know another escape route through a different set of hallways.

"Where's she going now?" Sam asked.

Nancy panted. "I have no idea. But we're about to find out."

After trailing Pia down dark corridors, Nancy and Sam came to a bank of elevators. Pia was already in one, and the doors shut on her and a very frightened Esme just as Nancy and Sam approached. From the lights displayed above the elevators, Nancy saw that this bank was an express to the hotel's penthouse.

Nancy pushed the call button. "Ready for another ride?" she asked as another elevator descended for them. "Looks like we're headed for the roof this time."

Just as the elevator doors were closing, a group of security guards arrived. "Reinforcements," Sam said to them. "See you at the top!"

When the elevator reached the top floor, Nancy spotted Pia tearing down the hallway. "We've got her trapped," Sam said through gritted teeth.

At the end of the hall, Nancy and Sam came to a staircase that led to the roof. From the bottom of the stairwell, Sam called up, "Pia, it's useless. We have you trapped."

"I don't think she's going to listen to reason," Nancy said. With that, she took the stairs, two at a time.

On the roof a cold blast of wintry air hit Nancy. Against the backdrop of River Heights' nighttime lights, Nancy saw Pia, backed up against a low wall at the roof's edge, with Esme pressed against her.

"Don't come any closer," Pia warned. "Or else I'll take us both over."

"We won't hurt you," Nancy assured the woman. "Why don't you tell us what you want?"

From behind Esme, Pia's face was a pale shadow, but her eyes flashed madly as she focused on Nancy and Sam. "I want her to admit that she lied," Pia asserted.

"About what?" Sam asked.

"Please let me go," Esme wailed. "I never lied about anything."

"That's not the point," Pia said viciously. "You lied about our book. You stole the manuscript of *Black Widow*. You told me you couldn't get it published, but you did. I was watching, I saw exactly what you did. You waited, but after a while, when you thought I wouldn't remember, you went ahead and published it under a different title. That was my work, too, and you stole it from me. And then you took all the credit. Admit it. Admit you lied to me."

"I never stole *Black Widow*," Esme protested. "I don't know what you're talking about."

"Pia." Nancy took a step forward. "I'm sure we can work this out. It sounds like you and Esme had a misunderstanding."

"Don't come any closer," Pia warned. She held the gun to Esme's side. "I just want her to admit she lied, then I'll let her go. I wanted to hear her say it in front of all those people, I wanted her adoring fans to hear it. Just like I wanted them to know that *Telling All* was a pack of lies, too."

"Were you the one calling Brenda Carlton?" Nancy asked.

Pia nodded. "That was me, all right. And I phoned in on the 'Emily Wells Show,' too. For years I've kept the truth about Esme to myself, but the time has come for all her adoring fans to know. If that meant ruining her career, then so be it."

"We were partners," Esme wailed. "How could you do this to me?"

"If you had come clean and admitted the truth, then I wouldn't have gone to such lengths," said Pia. "I wouldn't have had to steal your manuscript and scare you with that poisoning stunt. Didn't you see that if you'd just admitted to your lies, it all would have stopped?"

Somehow, Nancy didn't believe that Pia would have stopped—not until she had crushed Esme completely. "You're the liar!" Esme cried, turning on her former partner with a burst of strength and freeing herself from Pia's grasp. *"Black Widow* wasn't publishable. The next book that came out was my own work, and only my work. You had nothing to do with it!"

"That book stole every good idea from *Black Widow,* and you know it!"

Pia raised her arm to strike Esme, who rushed to defend herself. Nancy and Sam both saw the opening at the same time. In a flash, they were across the roof and at Pia's side.

Nancy came at Pia with her hands poised. Sam had his fists raised. When Pia saw that they were both coming at her, she backed away from Esme, who dropped to the ground. Pia prepared to defend herself.

"Good luck," Sam said through gritted teeth. "You'll need it."

Nancy lashed out with a kick to Pia's knee. The woman crumpled to the ground. Nancy approached, on guard against any fast moves. Pia lunged at Nancy, the gun poised, but Nancy was ready. With a swift jab from her right hand, Nancy chopped Pia's arm at the wrist. The woman fell back with a moan.

Sam grabbed at Pia's wrist, wrestling the gun out of her grasp. In the next move Sam wrapped Pia's arms behind her back. "Don't move if you know what's good for you," he commanded.

Seeing that Pia was disarmed, Nancy gently took Esme's arm and asked, "Are you okay? Did she hurt you?"

Esme's green eyes were full of fear and dismay. "I'm fine," she said. She took a deep breath. "You know something?" she continued with a fluttery smile, "I'm glad." She looked up at the clear night sky, and her breath came out in noticeable gasps.

"You are?" Nancy asked.

"Yes," said Esme. Her eyes trailed to Pia, standing now by Sam's side. "Finally this ordeal has ended. Thanks to you two, my life has been returned to me—safely."

An hour later Esme, Todd, Janine, Kim, Bess, Nancy, and Sam were standing by the refreshment table at the back of the ballroom. Esme had come back to her audience and explained to everyone the incident with Pia. Sam had called his backup, who had come to take Pia away. Soon, Esme would go down to the station to press charges against Pia. Now, Esme shivered at the memory of what she had been through.

"From the moment Pia learned about my autobiography," Esme explained, "she began to relive her animosity toward me."

"Especially since it reminded her of how far you'd come and where she was," Nancy said.

Bess's blue eyes went from Nancy's to Sam's to Esme's in wonder. "I can't believe Pia let her jealousy of Esme take over her life like that. She must have realized she'd get caught eventually."

"I don't think she cared," Sam put in.

Giancarlo took Nancy aside for a moment. "I want you to know," he said in his softly accented voice, "that after all this has quieted down, I plan to leave Esme."

Nancy pretended to be surprised. "But you love each other so much."

Giancarlo put his finger to his mouth. "That is how it appears. In truth, Kim and I love each other. That note was meant for her, and I have been trying to find a way to tell Esme. Now, I think I will be able."

"Esme will miss you very much," Nancy said. She and Giancarlo looked back to the group and saw that Todd had his arm around Esme's shoulders.

"Perhaps," said Giancarlo. "Perhaps she has found that she, too, loves someone else."

"You may be right," said Nancy, returning to the group.

Esme put her hand on Todd's arm. "I'd appreciate it if you'd come with me to the police station," she told him. "This won't be very pleasant, and it would feel good to have an old friend there."

Bess shot Nancy a meaningful look. Somehow, it all made sense. Nancy had seen firsthand that Esme still had a soft spot in her heart for Todd. Maybe the fact that she and Sam had found out about Giancarlo had made Esme think twice about her arrangement with her Italian leading man. Or maybe it was the clear evidence, so obvious to all by now, that Giancarlo really did like Kim and was trying his best to find a way to tell Esme.

"Romance is most definitely in the air," Nancy said to Bess.

The strains of music came drifting over. On the floor, carefree couples danced. Sam came to stand by Nancy and Bess and put his hand on Nancy's arm. "You're telling me," Bess said, edging away.

"That was great teamwork," Sam said, staring deeply into Nancy's eyes.

"You're right," said Nancy, returning his gaze. Suddenly it was as if they were completely alone, even though Esme was still there, along with Janine, Todd, Bess, Kim, and Giancarlo. All Nancy could hear was the music coming from the end of the ballroom, and all she could see were Sam's chocolate brown eyes, focused on her.

"So what do you think?" Sam asked.

"About what?" Nancy returned.

"About working together in the future?"

"I'm going to have to ask my heart," Nancy replied. "Right now, it's telling me not to decide, just to let everything take care of itself."

Sam smiled gently. "I was hoping for something more definitive, but I guess I can live with that for now." He gave Nancy's hand a squeeze. Nancy thought this might be the start of another kiss, but Bess came over before anything could happen.

"Boy, have you missed some fireworks," she

announced breathlessly. "Janine just admitted that she was the one to tip off Brenda to the spider incident."

"She did?" Nancy asked, surprised.

Bess nodded. "She only admitted it because Kim kept insisting Janine was Brenda's anonymous source. You should have seen Janine explode! She claims that she didn't call Brenda that first day, and she wasn't the one to warn her about what would happen at Esme's reading. But she did reveal the news about the spider. I guess she thought it would keep the PR train going. Esme got pretty mad, but I don't think she's going to fire her."

Nancy laughed. "Bess, what will you do when you don't have an inside track on all this gossip?"

At first Bess looked perplexed, then her face brightened. "Oh, I'll be plenty busy," she said. "I plan to write my own romance novel, remember? After everything that's happened, I figure I have enough material for years to come!"

Nancy's next case:

Ever since working on a case with handsome River Heights detective Sam Fanelli, Nancy has wanted to get to know him better. But not like this, not under these circumstances. They've come together once again to work on an investigation—one that could prove both painful and perilous: the kidnapping of an eight-year-old boy! Third-grader Jeremy Wright is caught in a custody battle between his movie star mother and paternal grandfather. In the midst of the legal disputes, Jeremy disappears. Nancy and Sam know that the urgency and danger are growing by the minute. And time is running out fast: one of their top suspects has been found . . . murdered . . . in *Stolen Affections,* Case #105 in The Nancy Drew Files™.